The Yibir of Las Burgabo

Mahmood Gaildon

The Red Sea Press, Inc.
Publishers & Distributors of Third World Books

P.O. Box 1892   P.O. Box 48

Trenton, NJ 08607   Asmara, ERITREA

The Red Sea Press, Inc.

Publishers & Distributors of Third World Books

P.O. Box 1892 P.O. Box 48

Trenton, NJ 08607   Asmara, ERITREA

Copyright © 2005 Mahmood Gaildon

Cover design: Ashraful Haque
Book design: Roger Dormann

Library of Congress Cataloging-in-Publication Data

Gaildon, Mahmood.
 The Yibir of Las Burgabo / Mahmood Gaildon.
   p. cm.
 ISBN 1-56902-218-6 (cloth) -- ISBN 1-56902-219-4 (pbk.)
1. Somalia--Fiction. 2. Children--Fiction. 3. Fathers--Death--Fiction.
4. Brothers and sisters--Fiction. I. Title.
 PS3607.A359Y53 2005
 813'.6--dc22

              2004028637

Dedication

I dedicate this novel to three men who have had the greatest impact on my intellectual and professional maturity.

Professor Allan Blaer—a teacher of unimaginable talent and dedication—made Columbia University's physics department a home to me for many years. Dr. Lowell Anderson of Memorial Sloan-Kettering Cancer Center—the preeminent brachytherapy physicist of his time—granted me my first job in the field of medical physics and mentored me through difficult times. In the late Mohamed (Dalab) Abdillahi Sugulleh, who taught me history and geography in intermediate school, I found an intellectual role model and enduring inspiration. I miss him.

Allan, Lowell and Mohamed, thank you for being there.

Acknowledgements

A number of people have in their own ways, and through their collective effort, made this book a reality.

Without wife Zeinab's understanding and devotion, I could not have spent countless hours writing and revising the novel. Our six lovely children (Asiya, Abdurahman, Ali, Abdalla, Alia, and Ahmad) have had to forfeit quality time with Daddy and exciting time on the computer. But by the looks on their faces when they learnt Daddy had a book on the way, I knew the exercise was not in vain.

I am indebted to publisher Kassahun Checole for accepting my manuscript for publication. Staff editor Angela Ajayi provided me with guidance on style and cheered me on in daunting times. Said M.M. Shireh was a motivator and a resourceful reference. Still, my utmost appreciation and gratitude go to Professor Ali Jimale Ahmed (Queens College, New York) whose critical commentary gave the novel much of its focus and depth. In fact, Professor Ahmed's role was so crucial that it is safe to say that without his support the book would have most likely never seen the light of day.

As it takes a village to raise a child, it takes a dedicated team to present a new book to the world. Thanks to all involved.

Prologue

A long time ago, Bu ur Ba ayr, the patriarch of Yibirs, challenged Yousuf Al-Kawneyn, the most prominent Muslim sheik among Aji Somalis, to a duel in which each would demonstrate his supernatural powers. Bu ur Ba ayr split a mountain, stood in the fissure, and then challenged the sheik to match his feat. The sheik had the two halves of the mountain collide, thereby killing Bu ur Ba ayr. To settle their ensuing conflict, Yibirs and Ajis went into a solemn social contract. Thereafter, Yibirs would receive a token payment for each baby boy born to an Aji family.

—Somali myth

Chapter 1

Orphaned

He found the door ajar when he came home. He pushed it in and stepped inside. The door swung to, creaking as it did so. Hungry and tired, he called to his sister to ask for food, but there was no answer. He moved forward. Two gingerly steps later, he stumbled on her lying on her side, her chin almost touching her knees.

"Amina, Amina," he said softly. But there was still no reply.

He could tell she was alive because he could see the up and down heaving of her torso as she breathed. *She must be sick*, he thought and squatted next to her, running his trembling hand over her forehead, a gesture he had learned from his father. She opened her eyes and looked at him strangely then let out a piercing scream, "Our father is dead!"

Ali found the shrillness of the cry and the state of his sister more appalling than the actual news. He looked at Amina, as if to say, but it is you I am worried about. Her tousled hair, contorted face, and red eyes gushing with tears were too much for him to bear. Nine years younger, he loved her dearly and looked to her as a child would to a mother. He had never seen her cry before, and now she was wailing uncontrollably.

"Stop crying. Please, stop crying," he begged her tearfully.

Oblivious to him, she continued wailing, beating her chest and the floor with her palms. Occasionally, she held her head in her hands and nodded up and down.

Ali felt utterly powerless. He rose to his feet and took a few steps toward the corner of the room. But feeling giddy, he quickly took two uneasy steps back and then collapsed next to his sister. He, too, cried aloud now out of helplessness and fear.

Suddenly, Amina stopped her own wailing and looked at him.

She rubbed her eyes and took another look at him. The sight of her brother writhing and crying jolted her. She had an impulsive urge to console him. Quickly and with the zest of an anxious mother, she grabbed him and held him close. Gradually, they both calmed down, and she was able to pause and take stock of the situation. Then, as if divinely inspired, she rose to wash her face in the bathroom. When she returned, she gave him a wide but affected smile, in the first footsteps of her role as the comforter of a child who could not yet grasp the gravity of the situation before them.

The deceased, Geeddi, had doted on his two children and spent considerable time with them. He even braved social norms and sent Ali to school, at a time few parents thought much of school. It did not occur to him that Amina, too, would need to go to school. A girl's place was home, most parents believed.

Geeddi's connection with his daughter was, nevertheless, special. Unlike Ali, Amina and Geeddi knew what all three of them had lived through years earlier. And the two, father and daughter, colluded to protect little Ali from the secret they guarded carefully. "Too young!" the father would say of Ali. "Too young!"

On a cool October day in the year 1970, the Yibirs of Somalia's northern town of Las Burgabo gathered in Geeddi's house to mourn his death. They had known him as an eccentric fellow. A tenaciously independent man and something of a lone wolf, he talked little and worked hard. But more than anything else, it was the steely resolve etched on his face that set him apart. He managed to crack a smile now and then; but one could always detect some measure of bitterness. Some liked him, others didn't. But they all respected him for his dignity and sense of independence, and they were now truly saddened to learn of his death.

First came the women, looking as if the end of the world were near and all would soon perish. Soon the fragrance of burning incense dominated the air. Two teenage girls brought blankets, pillows, mats and utensils and bustled about to ready the house for mourning. Food had been prepared in other Yibir houses and brought in. Meanwhile, more women stole into the house, as if careful not to disturb sleeping ghosts, and joined the others. Some held their heads in their hands and wept silently, while murmuring verses of the Koran. Others looked up, as if to God, and swayed from side to side, lamenting with a keen.

Ali found the sudden change disconcerting. To him, home had always been a refuge from the outer world. He had seen the door as a sharp divide between a comforting inside and a mysterious outside that made him ill at ease. But now strangers had taken over the house and turned him into a timorous spectator.

He became deaf to the bizarre dramatization being enacted in the house. It confused him. Two of the women had hugged him and planted multiple kisses on his delicate, tear-stained cheeks. The rest had passed him by as they came in, with little notice or acknowledgment. A buck-toothed old woman seemed to be either on the verge of falling forward or ready to spring up. Ali cowered in a corner of the room, not knowing what to do or how to behave. One woman seemed to be gazing at him all the time. Another had fallen to her side and buried her face in her hands, making it hard to tell whether she was sleeping or crying. At one point, the woman who gazed at him whispered to the one sitting next to her, who in turn whispered to another. Suddenly, all the women were staring at him anxiously.

What have they seen on me? Ali wondered. He stood up like a deer smelling danger and looked about nervously.

"He is in shock!" one of the women shouted.

Ali turned towards the door and made a move; but before he could bolt, three women lunged at him and held him like a prized catch. They then laid him down on his side, put a pillow under his head and covered him with a blanket. Turning his head and looking up, he beheld pairs of eyes staring down at him and lips moving speechlessly. He wished he could escape, but all he could do was yield and wonder when it would all end and when he would be free to sit, to stand, and to run again.

After dusk, the men arrived and sat cross-legged on mats laid outside the house. They sat in a circle and prayed. Wearing somber but defiant looks that betrayed no emotion, the older ones fingered prayer beads, as did some of the older women.

Las Burgabo's small Yibir community was repeating a ritual it had performed barely a month earlier, after a Yibir girl of fifteen had been raped and murdered. The Yibirs knew who the perpetrator was, but they chose to keep quiet. Then as in now, they mourned and moaned the Yibir's way: alone and quietly.

Ali, finally freed, sat with the men and watched their faces as he had watched the women's faces. One man had a long scar etched across his face, another had a cloven beard, a third had sharp, penetrating eyes. The man with the cloven beard tugged at one side of it, making Ali wonder when he would switch to the other side. To Ali, these large men with long limbs seemed to be angry. He felt small and frail sitting among them. But to his relief, the men, unlike the women, paid him no attention. Bored and tired, he wished he could be alone with his sister; but he did not have long to wait.

After food had been served, the oldest man in the group began to speak, and all fell silent. First, he called upon all to forgive the deceased, in case the deceased had offended any of the mourners or owed any a debt. Next, he turned to God:

"We all know he was a man of God—polite, honest, and kind to all of us. He touched all of us with his compassion. O Allah! Be kind to him and spare him Hell Fire. O Allah! Take him to Paradise and make the Prophets and the people of virtue his companions. O Allah! He has left his two children alone. O Allah! We beg for your benevolence to them. O Allah! Put them on the right path. O Allah! We thank you for your endless bounties, and remain humble before you and in need of your continued munificence and magnanimity."

The old man's words jolted Ali's mind to the meaning of the situation at hand. He listened carefully and watched the face of the old man, wondering whether he was in commune with God and with the soul of his father. He felt himself in the grip of a mysterious power that reached deep inside him and unnerved him and made him sick.

After the benediction, all the visiting mourners left save for two middle-aged women who would stay with Ali and Amina through-out the mourning period.

For seven days, the Yibirs gathered to repeat the mourning ritual every afternoon—the number of mourners gradually dwindling, then, on the seventh and final day, rising to the initial size. Henceforth, Ali and Amina would be left to grieve alone.

Amina was convinced that her father's death was tied to their tragic past. Her father, she believed, had not told her the truth about his fateful trip. She could read the signs. In his last few months, his nights had grown restless, his temper sharp and quick, his demeanor mournful—all signs that he was finally cracking under some immeas-urable yet potent strain. *Yes,* she thought, *the damned past reached back to claim his life.*

Amina's understanding of what had happened brought to life a sad chapter of her past and, thus, compounded her agony. Now, the painful secret of her family haunted her, tormenting her day and night, at a time when she had no one to turn to for solace.

To Ali, on the other hand, his father's death was yet another mys-tery in a world of mysteries. That the only parent he had ever known had departed earth so suddenly was an incomprehensible and terri-fying specter to him. A feeling that something horrible, painful, and irreversible had happened to his father weighed on him heavily. He felt abandoned, thrust into the unknown without guidance or protec-tion. His father had brought food to the house, nursed him when he was sick, and taught him many, many things. His father had been the biggest constant in his young life and the person he had felt most comfortable with. Emptiness, loneliness, anxiety, and the sense of being undeservedly deprived and denied were now constant com-panions.

Perhaps more significantly, he was now acutely aware of the mor-tality of things. Fear took the place of life, love, and pleasant dreams, and he saw the world as one fraught with danger. So he spoke little and communicated mostly through eyes that were sometimes blank, sometimes moist and beseeching, sometimes fear-stricken, but always more eloquent than the magic words of the finest poets.

On the day following the period of mourning, Ali woke up early. For the first time in more than a week, he and Amina were the only people in the house. Contrary to his previous desire for solitude, he now missed the mourners and thought fondly of them. He went into the bathroom and emerged in more confusion and sadness than when he entered.

Amina, on the other hand, was concerned with more immediate problems. Talking to herself, she lamented that she had not cleaned Ali's only set of school uniform. She almost decided to delay his return to school by a day before she handed him the dirty uniform. Ali put on the uniform, struggling as he did so, then sat on the floor, holding his head. He was unable to grasp or to make sense of their new situation.

"Don't do that! Please, don't!" cried Amina. "It isn't the end of the world."

She served him a breakfast of dry bread from the day before and a cup of tea that she had prepared before he woke up.

Out he came into a new and uncertain world, headed in the direction of the schoolhouse. The sun had not been up long enough to warm the cool October morning. He shivered slightly. Walking with unusual caution, he clutched his faded school bag, now more a weight than a badge of honor. About a hundred yards into his walk he stopped to reflect. Reflection changed into reverie, and he felt compelled to replay a scene. In his mind and in his soul, he felt the embrace and the kiss. Then, the agony of the parting was repeated, followed by a protracted melancholy gaze at the striding figure headed south and disappearing behind the hills. The child stared hard, as if by the force of his will alone he could travel back in time to be with his smiling father. But, alas, no! The forever-silent hills stood like a giant wall never to crack open, never to allow him to take even a peek.

After a while, Amina shouted and asked him what the matter was. Snapping out of the daydream, he turned around to take a look at her and found his vision blurred. He touched his cheeks and felt the wetness. Then he waved to her and continued his walk to school.

Now keenly aware of his distinctness from everything else, he observed his surroundings with a heightened sense of his individuality. Trees looked too tall, houses too large, men too strong. He stood out, he felt, as small, frail, and vulnerable, and he walked with caution.

Just before arriving at school, he wiped his eyes and his cheeks with his bare hands. He then headed to the principal's office to explain his one-week absence.

"What happened to him?" asked the principal.

Ali raised his right hand and meekly pointed south. "He died in a very faraway place," he said, his soft voice tapering off in a feeble whisper.

The principal put his hand on the child's head and prayed that Allah send Geeddi to Heaven. He had known Geeddi and admired his courage and wholeheartedly supported his high hopes for Amina and Ali. *Poor orphans! What will they do now?* the principal asked himself.

"Go to your classroom, and let me know if you have any problems. Your father was a good man, and I know you will be a good boy."

The news of the death of Ali's father spread among his classmates on the first day of his return to school. They could not talk to him about his father's death, superstitiously believing death was a taboo. But in their own way all the children showed sorrow and understanding by talking to him and touching him and laughing and playing with him.

Yet the next day brought with it a strange twist. Ali's classmates avoided him. They talked in hushed tones and from time to time glanced at him sideways to make sure he could not hear them. Ali hated the quick, furtive looks and the whispers that excluded him. He knew he was being rejected and frozen out, but he could not understand why. Ignoring the cold treatment, he sidled up to his classmates now and then, only to see them scatter away.

The open rejection befuddled him, especially on the heels of the warmth and succor he had received the day before. He did not know what to make of it, although he felt it was somehow connected to his father's death. Did death show on him? Was he doomed? He felt angry and humiliated and lonely, and he restlessly sat and walked about with a hangdog look. But he fought the urge to cry.

Finally, and after what seemed to be a particularly long day, the bell rang and Ali walked home. He was so weak both mentally and physically that he could barely carry his bag or think clearly. But he could feel, and he felt in abundance. He had never been so badly treated by his classmates when his father was alive. His father had been his source of life, fountain of knowledge, tower of strength, and link to the outside world.

He saw death as the sinister force that had spirited his father away. For the first time, he began to think of death with a deep sense of bitterness. As he saw it, death did not just snatch his father away; death replaced his father. His father had been an omnipresent force in his life, providing him with a blanket of security. Now it was death that was omnipresent in his life. Death dominated his psyche and put him in an almost delusional state. He saw death in the wind, death in the woods, death in the dust, death in the shadows, death everywhere. Yet death did not threaten him with death. Death stalked him and taunted him and continually reminded him that it was his nemesis in life.

When Ali reached home, he was in a fog, and Amina could see his weary look and glazed eyes. He walked past her and sat on his mat.

"I am not going back to school," he declared.

Amina's jaws dropped, and her eyes fixed Ali with an intense stare.

"I don't want to hear that," she countered. "What happened at school? Tell me!" It was unthinkable to her that he could have a major problem at school while still in mourning.

Ali had to talk to her and explain the cause of his anguish. "They didn't talk to me. They moved away from me. I don't know what I did to them. The…They don't want me. They don't like me. I…I got no friends at school," he mumbled.

Amina understood what Ali was unable to understand, and she was offended and angry. For a moment she stood, as if frozen, and stared into space. Her father's words rang clear in her ears: "They will try to get in your way. Don't let them!"

She knew how much her father would have loved to see his son through school. "Learn, learn," he had urged his son, "and be better than them all!"

Educated people, she knew, lived better, had more power, and were held in higher esteem than those who did not know how to read or write. She wanted her brother to be somebody important some day. Maybe he could be a teacher or a clerk who knew how to type. Maybe he could walk with men of high regard. But there he was, imploring her not to send him back to school.

"If your classmates accept you, will you go back to school?"

Ali's eyes widened with incredulity. Unwilling and unable to utter the words she wanted to hear, he nodded his head yes.

"Stay here! I will be back," Amina commanded, forgetting that she had not even fed him.

She donned a worn-out pair of sandals, covered her hair with a scarf, draped her shawl over her shoulders and walked out in the direction of the school. In her first major test as the head of the family, she was acutely aware of the heavy load fate had dumped on her back. Amina had already reached a state of defiance in her response to her father's death, and she was not prepared to accept defeat. With anger and determination as her sole companions, she walked hastily towards the principal's office.

Her walk took on the aura of a soldier purposefully marching into battle. Her steps echoed the sonority of a deep-sounding African drum. Scenes of long ago with her mother and more recent ones with her father flashed by as she marched on. She had not yet sorted out in her mind what to say to the principal or how to say it. She only knew she could in no way let her brother be the victim of ages-old superstitions and prejudices. Her father would have wanted her to see Ali through school, something she was determined to do. No, she could not let them run her brother out of school. As she saw it, this was an emergency she had to attend to. She had to take a stand and act.

At the school, Amina was directed to the principal's office. Her pace slowed considerably as a wave of doubt and anxiety stole over her, taking the place of her resolve and sense of purpose. No longer able to remain cloaked in the skin of a rugged adult, she reverted to the child she was. She took the last few steps to the door and then stood to gather her breath and thoughts. She knocked once then hesitated, her hand suspended in midair, before she knocked a second time.

"Come in," a man's voice said.

She opened the door slowly, put one foot inside, and then paused as if to test the ground's solidity. She took the other foot and placed it inside. Feeling disoriented and out of place, she steadied herself against a wall and stood still.

The principal was leafing through a large book on his desk. A minute or two later, he looked up and was surprised to see a poorly dressed young woman who was not one of his students.

"What can I do for you?" the principal asked, regarding her inquisitively.

She looked back at him with teary eyes and attempted to talk, but her pursed lips could only quiver.

"Please, sit down," the principal directed her, pointing to a chair, "and take your time. I'm in no hurry." He could tell she had come for help in a gravely important matter.

Amina took her time composing herself. Then, in a quivering voice, she blurted out, "Our father said you were different from the others."

This was not how she had intended to start; it simply came out of her mouth.

The principal was a man of about thirty years, but he looked considerably older. Tall and slightly bulky, he carried his weight exceedingly well. A bushy beard and a thick mustache dominated a round, fleshy face that was at once relaxed and intense. His eyes beamed, exuding confidence, vitality, and intellectual curiosity at the same time. A strong, resonant voice—which he used deftly in his captivating eloquence—complemented his imposing physique and gave him a commanding presence. Within the span of a single sentence, he could vary his voice in volume, cadence, and tone, along with his facial expression, to a mesmerizing effect. He was the type of a speaker who seemed to lock onto the minds of his audience and inspired them to think and learn more. No wonder students were in awe of him and came away from his lectures with a strong sense of motivation, optimism and confidence.

He had been among the first groups of Somali students sent to the United States for college education. An ardent African nationalist even before he traveled to the USA, he was caught up in the civil rights movement of the sixties. He initially worked with a group of radical black activists with violent tendencies but soon abandoned militancy in favor of passive resistance. Though convinced that Malcolm X, the militant black nationalist, better articulated the grievances of the black masses in America, he was persuaded by the nonviolent methods of Dr. Martin Luther King. He traveled to different cities and college campuses. He took part in marches and demonstrations, and disseminated propaganda. He immersed himself in books on civil rights and national liberation movements. Consequently, he had little time to study and graduate before his four-year scholarship ended. He, therefore, had to return to Somalia without a diploma to show for his long sojourn in America.

Back in Somalia, the Ministry of Education recognized and appreciated his pedagogical possibilities well enough to employ him as a teacher. Having mellowed considerably by then, he was ready to take his formal responsibilities seriously. His collection of books was shipped to him, and all he wanted was a relatively small town where he could indulge his passion for reading and for educating young people without distractions. To his relief, the Ministry of Education sent him to Las Burgabo, a town distant from the country's governmental and political machinations. He soon developed into so superb an educator that by the time Ali started school, he was in charge of the towns' heterogeneous system of elementary, intermediate and secondary schools. This was the man before whom Amina now stood and sought help.

Our father said you were different from the others echoed in the principal's head before it dawned on him that she was little Ali's sister.

Geeddi had told him a number of times that he had a teenage daughter who, though clever, had never been to school. *This must be she*, the principal concluded. Moved by her condition and thinking that she had come to seek financial help, he tried to console her.

"It will be all right. I will see what I can do. I will talk to people. Have faith in God. He ordains, and He shall not forsake either of you."

Amina's diffidence quickly gave way to a show of steely confidence tinged with quiet indignation. Mindful of how her father had been too proud to beg for charity, Amina found the principal's statement insulting.

"It isn't what you think," she shot back. She was now ready to plead her case forcefully.

"Today, Ali's classmates refused to talk to him. He doesn't want to go to school anymore," she complained. "I know why," she continued. "Those children are scared. They think a *hanfaley*[1] snatched our father. But I can't blame them. Grownups stuffed garbage into their little heads. They always do that when we lose someone and we can't show the body. I hate it."

Amina's sudden change of demeanor startled the principal and put him at loss for words. He looked down and frowned in intense concentration before he was able to answer.

"They really did that?" the principal asked in exclamation. "I'm really sorry for what happened. You are...right," he added, "it is...unfortunate that we have to deal with such nonsense."

Stroking his beard, he thought for a moment and then added, "Tomorrow, let Ali stay home. I will have a chat with his classmates."

Relieved but uncertain as to exactly what she had just accomplished, Amina thanked the principal and rose to her feet to leave. But before she reached the door, the principal asked her about her and Ali's financial situation. Amina lowered her eyes and kept silent. The principal then reached into his pocket, took out a wallet and offered Amina a one-hundred-shilling bill.

---

[1] In Somali mythology, hanfaley is an evil force thought to snatch and spirit away Yibırs at the time of death.

The principal's kindness caught Amina so off guard that for a moment she did not know what to do or say. She stood motionless and gazed at him, as he stood towering over her. Then she extended a trembling hand and, over the objections of her dead father, took the money. For the first time in her life, Amina accepted money from someone other than her father. She saw it as a gift from God.

She stepped out of the principal's office with much more bounce than when she had entered. The principal's generosity and goodwill towards her gave her a dose of optimism about the future—after all, the world was not as cruel as she had feared. She was now confident that the principal would find a way to make the school a hospitable place for her brother. Her first major test had just ended successfully. Looking up, she saw the fleecy autumn clouds racing through the sunny and clear sky. It was well past lunchtime. She quickened her pace.

When she reached home, Amina found Ali in a deep sleep with his sandals on.

"Woe onto me," she lamented, "I have almost killed him." She stepped into the kitchen, checked the pot of plain rice and discovered that part of the food was gone. She gasped with surprise and smiled. Ali had not only fed himself, but he had also washed the cup and the plate he had used. This was a big accomplishment for a boy of his age in a society where all males relied on mothers, sisters, wives, and daughters to do the menial work. Helping himself in the kitchen was a sure sign that Ali was beginning to recognize and adjust to the new situation correctly. She moved back into the main room, took Ali's sandal's off, and opened a window, hoping to make it cooler for him. She then knelt next to him and kissed him on the forehead and prayed, "May Allah spare you all misfortune. May you rise above all other boys."

He stirred and turned on his side.

The *muezzin* called the faithful to afternoon prayers, his voice rising and falling with the wind. After prayers, Amina took an old, heavily encrusted, blackened kettle, rinsed it out, and half-filled it with water. Next, using charcoal, she built a fire and made tea. Ali, now awake and sitting opposite her, noticed Amina's animated and brisk moves. She poured him a cup of hot tea and poured herself one. Facing each other and sitting on the bare dirt floor, they sipped tea. For a time neither said a word, and all that could be heard was the sibilant sipping of tea through barely parted lips. The tea was sweet and fragrant, and Ali felt its refreshing warmth travel down to his stomach. He looked into his sister's face and saw a brightness he had not seen since the calamity. Their eyes met. He smiled. She giggled. Then he started to giggle too but stopped short, looking hurt.

"What's the matter?" she asked.

Relaxing his face a little, he attempted a smile. It came out feebly and fleetingly. She looked at him and studied his face.

"Let's go outside. We will visit some people," Amina said.

They stepped outside and walked towards the town. The short and narrow streets were now coming back to life. They avoided passing in front of teashops, because Amina's female modesty would not allow her to be seen by the men sitting outside. They took side streets. A man goaded a donkey loaded with large tin cans of water. Unable to walk fast enough for his master's liking, the poor donkey kept getting poked. A shirtless old porter carried a large gunnysack of charcoal as a stronger and much younger man followed closely. Little bare-footed boys wearing shorts kicked a ball around in a small dusty field under the clear blue sky. Some looked at Ali and giggled.

Stopping to watch the boys, Ali noticed their festive mood. The ball bounced up and down and from side to side. He stood still and watched as if bewitched.

"Let's go!" urged Amina. But finding him unresponsive, she pulled him by the arm and led him away.

They walked through different parts of the town until they came to an area of squalid huts very similar to those near their house. They stopped in front of one such hut. Before Amina could knock on the door, one of three women chatting under an acacia tree rose to her feet and walked towards them. Ali recognized her as Awrala, the buck-toothed old woman he had seen at his father's mourning. This time she wore a happy face. She smiled and greeted them, then knocked on the door and called for her daughter to open it. A girl of about twelve opened the door and stood aside.

Never had Ali seen such squalor. Everything around him was dirty. The young girl, Maryam, was in slimy rags, and her mother's clothes were equally slimy and threadbare. A foul odor, vaguely evocative of animal skins and putrid milk, hang about the house. Yet both mother and daughter appeared happy. The girl looked at the visitors, then tilted her head jauntily and smiled modestly. A vague but unmistakable sense of comfort came over Ali.

"What are you waiting for?" asked Awrala a little harshly, addressing her daughter. "Go and make tea for the guests!"

Maryam withdrew to prepare the tea, which she served to all except herself. Awrala apologized for the lack of milk. She and Amina chatted and laughed over tea, from time to time involving the youngsters in their conversation. Ali learned that Awrala's husband Musse spent most of the day stacking dried skins in a warehouse, and that Awale, their twenty-year old son, dug pit toilets. Even at his tender age of nine, it was not lost on Ali that the trades of both father and son were considered ignoble and demeaning.

Just as Amina and Ali were preparing to leave, Awaleh came in, bearing six pieces of *kidar*[2]. Awrala insisted that Amina and Ali each have one. More tea was served to help wash down the hard and otherwise unpalatable kidar. Ali was not able to finish his piece, but the little he ate filled his stomach and assuaged his hunger. Then Amina and Ali had to leave so they could reach home before dark. They bid Awrala and her son and her daughter good night and stepped out. Awrala stepped out too and walked with them part of the way. The sun was about to set, the light was soft, a gentle breeze blew. Amina and Ali walked briskly and happily towards home.

When they arrived, Amina hurriedly performed her sunset prayers and then served Ali a glass of sour milk. He took a few sips before giving up.

---

[2] In parts of Somalia, a poor man's bread: small, hard and rough on the palate, and uneasy to swallow

"Drink! Drink!" Amina commanded. "How can you grow to be a man if you can't finish even a cup of milk?"

He tried again, taking a few more sips before giving up once more.

"Very well," said Amina, slowly shaking her head. "It will be here for you in the morning. You should know that sometimes we may not have even a cup of milk." She proceeded to pour the remaining milk back into the main milk container.

"You won't go to school tomorrow, but you will the day after. The principal will take care of things tomorrow, and you won't have to worry." There was a discernable touch of pride in making her major accomplishment of the day.

Just the mention of school made Ali squirm. He did not want a repetition of what he had gone through that day. But because he had learned to respect and obey his sister, he was not about to protest. He knew she could be quite stern.

"Go and wash your feet!" Amina ordered.

Ali obediently went to the bathroom to wash his feet. When he came back, it was time for storytelling. Amina knew many stories, and Ali enjoyed listening to them. He often wondered how Amina knew so many stories. He listened attentively and with great amusement, even though she had told him some of the stories many times before. Tonight she told him new stories and continued her narrative until she was sure he was sound asleep. She then moved to her own mat, sat down, and mused over past and happy times. She smiled sadly, then cried softly until she gradually calmed down and fell asleep.

The principal was on his way to address Ali's classmates. The task was a delicate one that would require a balancing act. On the one hand, he did not want to scold, nor did he want to inadvertently cast adults as villains for perhaps confusing the children. On the other hand, he did want to educate the children in the most unambiguous way.

He entered the classroom slowly. The pupils hushed, then stood up immediately. The principal bade them to be seated. They sat in rapt attention. The principal walked around, making sure he looked each student in the eye. His stern face gave clear evidence that he was about to address a very serious matter, but he showed no anger.

"It has been brought to my attention," he began, "that yesterday you froze Ali out. You didn't talk to him. I promise I won't punish you for this, but you should first be honest with me and speak without fear. Do you promise?"

His face breaking into an avuncular smile, he walked around, soliciting an answer from them one by one. The unanimous reply was, "Yes."

"Why did you reject Ali?" the principal asked.

One hand shot up. It was that of Fareh, the naughtiest boy in the class. The principal gave him permission to talk. In a soft voice belying his naughtiness, Fareh explained he had been told that a hanfaley had snatched Ali's father away, as it eventually would all Yibirs. Fareh cast his eyes down then up and added that he and others in the class were too frightened to stand or sit next to Ali. The hanfaley might swoop down on Ali and anyone sitting next to him. When Fareh finished, he gave the principal the look of a child in mortal fear of doom. The principal looked around and found the same expression on the faces of all the children.

Smiling and holding his arms wide, as if to hug them all, the principal declared, "My children, long ago someone attempted to create an amusing story. But, unfortunately, he came up with the story of the hanfaley, a scary one. We should all know that such tales hurt people and make their lives miserable. We hope that people like you will fight this superstition until it disappears. Now, I want you to trust me with this: There is no hanfaley."

The children seemed baffled, but their basic trust in their principal overcame their skepticism. Their principal was a father figure to them, and they loved him and were willing to trust him in this bizarre matter.

"Tomorrow," the principal proceeded, "Ali shall be back here, and you must all shake hands with him and apologize to him for the mistreatment you gave him yesterday. Do you promise?"

Nods and murmurs of assent reverberated in the classroom. Then the principal smiled, and all the children smiled back.

The meager supplies Geeddi had left Amina and Ali were dwindling to dangerous levels. The brother and sister would have to fend for themselves, especially since they had no close relatives in town, and other Yibirs were too destitute to help them. Amina would have to devise a means to earn a living. Had she been alone she could have attached herself to an *Aji*[3] family, as a servant little more than a slave, until she found a husband. It was going to be harder to support Ali; but support him she must for he was all she had by way of family. Silently but solemnly she vowed that, whatever happened, her major goal in life would be to care for Ali as best she could. And in due course, when he became a mature man, she would have to let him into the painful secret of their family's past. But first she would have to find a job. Her lack of schooling, her youth, her inexperience, and her Yibirness together presented a formidable obstacle. She decided to look for a job as a housemaid. It was time to face the world.

On the morning Ali would go back to school, Amina woke up early and took out the stove. (The stove was a cubic kerosene can with the top removed and a rectangular hole cut in one side. Crisscrossing blades—fitted through regularly spaced slits cut around the can about two inches below the top—formed a grid and a bed for the burning charcoal. The falling ashes collected at the bottom of the can and the gaping hole in the side helped circulate the air.) Amina filled the *girgireh*, as the stove was called, with charcoal, poured kerosene on the charcoal, and lit it, taking care to shield the nascent flames from the wind. When the coal started to burn, she fanned the flames through the gaping side hole until the fire could sustain itself.

Next, she prepared tea, and with a cup of tea in hand waited for the sun to rise. At sunrise, she placed a bucket of warm water in the bathroom and woke Ali up. He brushed his teeth, washed, and changed into his faded but now clean school uniform. Breakfast was composed of tea without milk and a few mouthfuls of boiled sorghum.

[3] The Aji are Somalis who consider themselves of noble birth. They constitute the overwhelming majority of Somalis. The Yibirs, the Midgans, and the Tumals, among several other groups, constitute the Sab.

When Ali set out for school, Amina started to prepare for her planned job hunt. She slipped into the same old dress and the same rugged and worn-out sandals and donned the same headscarf and the same shawl she had been wearing when she met the principal. She then headed for sections of the town inhabited by people she felt might have the means to hire her. Her plan was to go from house to house and ask for a job. Unlike her father, she had long come to terms with her painful past and learned to control her bitterness. She disciplined herself to talk to people and deal with them without the slightest betrayal of her deep-seated emotions.

Starting out around ten o'clock in the morning, when most housewives had returned from the market, she walked into town. At the open-air market, she stopped briefly on the unlikely chance she would meet someone who might help.

The market, a large walled area with trees and wooden benches, was bustling with people. Proud women in colorful garments milled around, baskets in hand, the free arms swinging rhythmically with their undulating gait. Fresh meat, including mutton, goat, beef, and camel, was displayed on the benches. Fresh vegetables and fruits were laid out on mats in the shade of acacia trees. Fresh camel milk, fresh cow milk, fresh goat milk, sour camel milk, sour goat milk, and tasty yogurts made from goat milk were brought into the market every few hours from the countryside. Women who could afford to buy as they pleased proudly displayed their purchases. Those of very limited means clung to their small baskets and slunk away as if in shame. Cacophonous sounds and voices filled the air: the clatter of vessels, the haggling over prices, the usual market chatter, and the heavenly laughter of the women.

Leaving the din of the market behind, Amina spent a significant portion of the day going from house to house asking for a job. The experience gradually turned sour and wore her down as she was turned away time and again. Some had momentarily raised her hopes high only to suddenly wax cold and shake their heads no when she told them she was a Yibir. Besides, she thought, her attire made her look like a pauper.

By noon she was tired and disappointed. She decided to call it a day and returned home in time to prepare lunch.

On the third day of her job search, Amina started out earlier than usual with the intention of canvassing a section of the town she had not been to. At midmorning, she knocked on a door and waited. She knocked again. Voices were coming from the house. She knocked a third time, and the door was opened. A middle-aged woman stood in the doorway and regarded Amina curiously. The woman's eyes ran over Amina, resting longer on her feet, then turned up to check her face.

"What do you want?" the woman asked.

"I am looking for a job as a housemaid," Amina answered.

"I don't need a housemaid," the woman snapped before she took a step back to close the door.

Amina turned and walked away. But a few steps later she heard, "Stop!"

She stopped and was surprised to see the woman walking towards her. A toddler bolted after the woman and clung to her arm. Looking up at Amina, the toddler grinned. Amina grinned back then, with quiet interest, waited for the woman to speak.

"Are you Geeddi's daughter?" the woman inquired, with a sense of serious concern. Amina gasped.

"Yes!" she replied. "Did you know him?"

The woman put her hand to her mouth, bit her index finger and, for a moment, gazed into space. "Of course," she said, "I knew him. What an honest and hardworking man! I heard about his death from our daughter. What those children did to your brother was bad, and I told my daughter so. It is good that he is back in school and things have changed. Oh! I almost forgot. You are looking for a job. Come back tomorrow. I will take you to a woman I know. But, first, change these sandals. Buy new ones... Oh! How stupid of me! ...Come in, and let me see your feet."

Dazed, Amina followed the woman into the house. The woman asked her to take her sandals off. Amina obliged, and the woman quickly concluded that Amina's feet were the same size as hers.

"Tomorrow, when you come back, I will give you a new pair of shoes and you will throw these away," said the woman, widening her eyes for emphasis and pointing a finger at the frayed sandals. Then she added, "Buy something for Ali with this," as she reached for and opened a small bag and handed Amina fifty shillings (at the time worth about eight U.S. dollars).

"May Allah reward you for your kindness to us. I will be here tomorrow. Thank you very much," said Amina, before she shook the woman's hand and walked out.

Feeling God's compassion and His guiding hand, Amina walked home. Hours later, she realized she had not even learned the kind woman's name.

The following morning, Amina headed straight to the woman's house, praying that the blessing would not slip away. She stood in front of the house, hesitant and wondering whether it might be too early. She stepped back. But then, as if on an impulse, she knocked on the door. The door flew open and the kind woman greeted her with a pleasant smile and open arms.

"Here you are! I was expecting you earlier," the woman said. "Please, sit down."

Amina sat. The woman went into another room and came back with a new pair of shoes.

"Put them on!" the woman urged Amina.

The shoes fit Amina's feet snugly, rendering her agog, as she had never before put her feet into shoes so comfortable and so beautiful.

"Now, come with me!" said the woman, elated by Amina's excitement.

The two women rose to their feet, and the woman led Amina to another house. On the way, they learned each other's names. The woman's name was Shukri. She had three sons and two daughters. Shukri told Amina that they were going to visit a woman who lived in a nearby spacious house with her three children, aged eight and younger. The woman, Sahra , worked as a clerk for the municipality, and her husband worked and lived in England.

Amina and Shukri, now talking like old friends, arrived at the house and were greeted by a very pretty and charming woman in her midtwenties. As it was Friday, the Muslim Sabbath, the woman did not have to go to work. She showed immediate interest in Amina, and they quickly struck a deal over tea. Amina was to report to work at six-thirty every morning, including Fridays. She would take a break between twelve and two o'clock in the afternoon, then come back and continue to work until six. She was going to be the housemaid, and she could start the following day. After making the deal, the three women chatted until Amina had to leave.

As Amina walked home, the world suddenly looked bright. Her feet felt light and nimble. The corners of her mouth twitched in a vain attempt to contain a burgeoning smile. The sun and the trees, the walls of the houses, and the birds on the trees and those flying high in the sky, and even the people, all the people, looked radiant and friendly. She felt like dancing and singing and laughing, but she had to walk like a modest woman. At last, she would no longer have to worry about what Ali and she would eat the next day. No more sleepless nights! No more tears shed in the dark! Ali would grow up like a cheerful, normal child and would remain in school and learn a thousand things and would be a man of high standing one day.

Chapter 2

\\\\|//

Grief and Hope

The hanfaley incident passed, but Ali's psychological crisis did not end there. As time went on, the pain of his father's absence became more and more acute. He would never see his father, touch him, or speak to him again. Amina explained that their father was in heaven, where God cared for good people. But it was no solace to him that his father was having a good time in heaven. He and Amina needed their father alive and well here on earth.

If God takes those He likes and puts them in heaven, does it mean that He doesn't like those still alive? How do people die? Doesn't death come only to sick old people? My father wasn't even a hundred years old! Do all people go to heaven when they die? Even the bad ones? No, no. The bad ones go to hell…I know where heaven is. Heaven is above the clouds. It visits us when it rains and becomes nice and cool. The rainbow comes from heaven. That is why it is so beautiful. Heaven is where my mother is.

I have never seen my mother. My father told me she was a good mother. But nobody says what happened to her. Amina doesn't want to talk about it. The last time I asked my father, he didn't want to talk about it either. He just told me to pray for my mother, which I do a lot. Why has God taken my mother away from me? Every child I know has a father and a mother.

My sister tells me not to cry, but I can't control my tears. Sometimes my tears flow into my mouth. Tears feel warm and taste salty… I am crying now. I can't control my tears. But I have to wipe my eyes and my cheeks before other people see me. My sister cries too sometimes. I have seen her crying, though she tries to hide it from me. But I am a man. I am not supposed to cry. That was what my father used to tell me: "Be a man! Be a man!"

But it was not easy for Ali to "be a man." His grades plummeted and he lost a lot of weight. Initially his teachers thought his condition would blow over in a few weeks. But when it had dragged on for almost five months they began to worry. They were stumped and clueless as to what to do to help him. All they could do was watch him turn into a brooding wretch and a shadow of his former self.

The principal, though, was unwilling to give up on the bright boy who only a year earlier, in Grade II, had shown promise. He decided to visit Amina and Ali and have a serious talk with them. So one Friday afternoon, he walked from his house, located in the government part of town. It was mid-March just before spring, when temperatures were just beginning to soar. The air was still, as if bracing for the approaching rains, and the sky was clear.

Following the quickest way to the Yibir house, the principal walked down a slope and into the town. About a mile away to his left, he could see herds of camels and flocks of sheep and goats being given water at the wells. And he could hear the herdsmen singing. In the distance, a truck approached followed by a mound of dust.

Ten minutes later, the principal was in town. He passed the post office, an old whitewashed structure built in colonial times, and turned left to go along the town's main street. He then came upon a man slouching on a wooden chair outside a small corner house. He recognized the man as a fellow student who had lost his mind in America—one of a number of such cases. Addur, as the lunatic was called, stayed indoors most of the day and only ventured out in the afternoons or early evenings, when he sat on a wooden chair and listened to the radio. He was now sipping tea.

"*Assalamu Alaykum*, Addur," the principal greeted, " How do you feel today?"

Looking up, Addur strained his face and narrowed his eyes. He then gave a wan smile, murmured and went back into his lonesome and closed world. The principal could only shake his head in sympathy and proceed with his walk down the street.

Whenever he walked into town, the principal was often accosted and buttonholed by friends and acquaintances and even by people he did not know. People liked to chat with him, and he often spent a significant amount of time on these casual encounters in the middle of the street. Today, however, he walked with a more-than-usual sense of purpose and a quick pace, his heavy figure slightly swaying from side to side.

The teashops were starting to fill with boisterous crowds. The teenage waiters were bustling about, taking orders harshly and loudly. The principal exited the street at the far end and came upon a clearing with two opposing goal posts. A lone, large and shady acacia tree graced one end of the field. Young boys were playing in the field, some kicking a small rubber ball around. When the boys saw the principal, they stopped and looked at him like a disturbed pack of foxes. His face breaking into a wide smile, the principal waved without slowing down one bit. Then the boys, elated at the sign of approbation they had just received from their principal, giggled and waved back. Their teeth and eyes gleamed under the effulgent sun.

The principal walked through the dilapidated shacks of abjectly destitute people. He saw naked children, some standing, some sitting, others running around. Upon seeing him, some of the children dropped their lower jaws in bewilderment and gazed at him, as if he were an alien. Others let out bursts of laughter, which seemed out of place with their obvious privation. *Childhood innocence*, he thought, as he strained to not hold his nose. He felt sorry for the children, because he knew that few, if any, would ever read or even hold a book.

About fifty yards beyond the squalid shacks, he reached an open space between a garbage lot on one side and small gullies on the other. Nearly three hundred yards farther, alone and secluded, stood the house of the two young Yibirs. Scattered bones, cans, and bits of paper littered the area.

It was not lost on the principal that the trip from his residence through the main town and the shacks had taken him through the disparate socioeconomic levels of the town's inhabitants. Those who lived in the shacks had been grouped together by economic necessity. The location of the Yibir house, however, had been determined by the reality of rejection and prejudice Yibirs lived. An eerie feeling swept over him as he pushed forward.

A few steps from the house, the principal paused and looked. He found the house in remarkably better shape than the shacks he had just passed. Yet it had a weird quality about it. Forlorn and gloomy like an abused orphan, it stood waiting to be called in from the cold. Sadness gripped him, as he pondered why Geeddi had brought his family to this desolate area. He soon realized why.

Geeddi's choice of location for the house presented a modicum of sense and harmony to an existence devoid of sense and harmony. Violently torn away from his own society, Geeddi could never have felt at home among Aji Somalis. So the Yibir house was Geeddi's way of screaming, "To hell with you all!" And the garbage lot and the gullies served him as a rampart of sorts against a real and brutal world. Yet the house did not stand too far away to prevent Geeddi from making a living in the town and from sending his son to school.

Amina and Ali lived in a hut built of thatch and mud. Geeddi had built the house with his bare hands and with little outside help. He went to the nearby woods to cut branches from trees and dragged them over miles of rugged terrain. He had to cross an area covered with gullies and small hills before he emerged into the open grassland that ended at the northern bank of a watercourse. Without beasts of burden, he had no choice but to rely on his muscle and his brain. Occasionally, he received some help from other Yibirs in the town— men dragging branches, women drawing water from a well quite a distance away.

The main part of the house had only two rooms, one of which was used as both a kitchen and a storeroom. A few yards from the main frame of the house, Geeddi dug a pit toilet about five yards deep and built an enclosure around it. The resulting roofless outhouse served as a bathroom. An outer wall, the height of an average man, cloistered the two-room structure and the bathroom. This was the house Amina and Ali called home. This was the Yibir house.

The principal took the remaining steps to the house and knocked on the door. It was as though he had been standing before a sacred shrine. Slowly, the door was unlatched and pulled in. Not seeing anyone, the principal hesitated to step inside. But a moment or two later, he pushed the door wide open, and found Ali behind it.

Upon seeing the principal, Ali gasped, then recoiled. The principal's presence in the house was extraordinary, and Ali did not like to deal with extraordinary things. Few Ajis had ever come to their door. And if they did, it was for only brief periods of time. No Aji had ever entered their house. Yet, amazingly, the principal himself was in the house!

"Is your sister home?" asked the principal, smiling. He realized the little boy was stunned and disturbed.

"She…she will come back after sunset," replied Ali. At school, he liked his principal. But he now saw him as an intruder, and a big one at that.

"May I come in and wait for her?"

"Yes," replied Ali. Hesitantly, he led the principal into the house, then stopped in the middle of the room, his back towards the principal, shielding his discomfort.

"Ali," the principal said, "look at me!"

Ali turned around and looked up but was unable to meet the principal's eyes. He looked down and stared into a void. Though the two stood within a few feet of one another, there was an invisible but perceptible barrier between them.

The principal studied the room. Two mats covered with tattered sheets lay in opposite corners. A homemade box lay in another corner, and an ancient kerosene lamp hung by a wire from the ceiling. The simplicity of the setting, the calmness of the atmosphere, and the Spartan conditions gave the house a holy look and made it curiously inviting.

Humbled and in deep thought, the principal walked slowly towards one of the two mats. *Down and poor they are*, he thought, *but out and defeated they are not.* He then turned towards Ali and said, "I will stay until your sister comes back," as he took his sandals off and sat down on the mat.

Still troubled, Ali stood in the middle of the room, his head hanging, shoulders slouching, the corners of his mouth drooping, eyes turned down. The principal looked at him intently and thought. As reflected in the specter he presented, the young boy lived in a world of loss and agony, with no one to care for him except a sister who had little to offer besides love and tears. At that moment the principal had an impulse to somehow reach deep inside Ali to draw out his thoughts and feelings.

"Maybe you can tell me some stories," the principal said in a gentle and soothing tone to break the awkward silence.

But seeing that Ali still seemed at loss, the principal decided to tell a story first. As it had been many years since he had last told a story, the task was taxing his memory. He reminisced about his childhood in the countryside when, at night after the animals had been milked, the family gathered around a bonfire and chatted. Those were times when everybody, including his father, laughed and talked freely. And it was at those times that he learned the rich Somali language spoken in the countryside. It was also on those occasions that he heard many folktales. He remembered clearly and with relish the night he was taught how to count. For him the very sound of the figures themselves— one, two, three… eighty, ninety, one hundred— was musical and mysterious.

Yes, I should start with Dhegdheer, he thought. It was one story he remembered clearly. He started the story in his characteristic resonant voice.

The principal telling a story! Ali sat down cross-legged on the bare floor in the middle of the room. He liked stories. Stories were something he could relate to. And to hear the principal tell a story was quite amusing.

Midway through the story, the principal sensed Ali's demeanor changing. The woebegone look on his face began to vanish and a child's innocent smile began to take shape. When, towards the end of the story, the principal paused to recollect his tale, Ali was prompt to come to his rescue. By the time the principal came to the end, Ali joined him in a chorus of two: *Dhegdheer is dead, and the land is in peace.*

Then, it was Ali's turn. He decided on the story of *The Young Woman Who Married the Hyena*— and had a boy and a girl by it. Speaking softly, Ali related the story of the woman and her half-man-half-beast children's journey back to the human folk—an imaginative depiction of the unity between man and beast. The principal told the story of *Yunis the Thief*, whose ingenuity at thievery won him an enduring place in Somali lore. Ali told the story of *Igal Shidad the Coward,* who became famous for his amusing antics in trying to evade perceived dangers and his poetic explanations for his cowardice. The principal countered with the story of *Arraweelo*, the mythical queen of Somalia, and her campaign to literally castrate all males to eliminate potential threats to her crown. The queen is, in the end, brought down by a rebellion of geldings led by the two uncastrated males remaining in the land. Ali related the story of *Wil Wal*, a sultan known for his sharp wit and zealous search for wisdom. The sultan puts men and women through trying times and trickery to learn more about human behavior and to teach them.

Just before Ali finished the story of *Wil Wal*, Amina walked in and stood over the principal and his pupil in amazement. The presence of the principal in the house and in such a playful and childlike mood astonished her. Even more astonishing, however, was her brother's beaming face. Thank God, her brother was back!

Realizing that Amina had arrived, Ali paused, hesitating to continue.

"Don't stop!" Amina entreated. "Finish the story…I want to hear it too."

Without missing another beat, Ali proceeded to tell the whole story, as the principal and Amina listened. When he finished, he looked at his sister eagerly. A blissful sensation suffused her heart and imbued her face with an expression of joy and excitement. She applauded breathlessly.

The principal turned to take a look at Amina. He saw a tall and baby-faced beauty. Her chin thrust forward, lips locked tight, eyes at once serious and serene, neck upright, back straight, arms akimbo, she struck a proud and defiant posture. Yet, the principal could also see that behind the defiance and the pride stood a nubile, young woman. His gaze stayed on her; and the next time she looked at him, their eyes met and locked for a fleeting moment. It seemed to him as if a veil had just been lifted off her face. His Adam's Apple moved, and there was a flicker in both their eyes. Amina blushed and smiled nervously.

"You got a guest in the house and you offered him nothing, not even a cup of water!" Amina complained to her brother playfully, her voice sounding husky. She moved towards the kitchen.

"I will make tea," Amina declared.

"You don't have to. I won't stay long anyway," the principal protested.

"No! You got to have tea before you leave," insisted Amina.

The principal knew that it would be imprudent to refuse. He stayed and gladly accepted the hot cup of tea Amina presented to him. Sipping the tea in silence, he thought about and marveled at Amina's air of serenity and the loving and delightful way she looked at Ali whenever she addressed him.

After the principal finished his tea and performed sunset prayers, he decided it was time to deal with the purpose of his mission. He had planned to have a long and serious talk with Amina about Ali's deteriorating condition. Now, however, that he sensed the storytelling had produced a positive effect on Ali, he decided to use only light-hearted measures. Mindful not to disturb the prevailing cheerful mood, he asked Amina what Ali did from the time he came from school to the time he went to bed.

"After school…," said Amina, "After school…"

"After school, what?" asked the principal.

"After school, I give him lunch and then…"

"And then what?"

Only silence followed. Suddenly, Amina was wary. Her eyes assumed a cold, withdrawn dull look. Deep-seated emotions had taken the place of her initial excitement. She blew hot and cold between the instinctive desire to play the graceful hostess and the ingrained habit to be cautious and skeptical. Her father had told her the principal was different from the others. Besides, she was grateful to him for the way he had treated her when she met him in his office. Yet some inner voice told her not to open up. He was just too close. He had invaded their home, their sacred sanctuary, the house their father had built with his own hands.

The principal looked at the two with renewed interest. Amina and Ali, young and orphaned as they were, presented an impregnable fortress. These two seemingly fragile children were in reality powerful agents of a world that had immunized itself against Aji intrusion. The inability to communicate effectively frustrated the principal. He struggled to find a way to penetrate the cover of darkness that cloaked them.

He turned to Ali and asked, "Do you do your homework?"

"Yes," Ali said in a prompt response.

Aimina's eyes sparkled, and she threw her brother a commendatory look. She then turned to the principal with a conciliatory face. Her rigid façade softened, and she could no longer keep him at bay.

"Do you check his homework?" the principal asked, seizing the opportunity.

"Never been to school myself. I can't read or write. No, I can't check his work."

The principal was embarrassed because he had forgotten that Amina was illiterate.

"Then what happens after homework?" he asked.

"I give him whatever food I got at the time—a little bread, boiled sorghum, milk, sometimes only tea, sometimes a handful of dates, sometimes nothing. Then I tell him stories until he sleeps."

"Doesn't he have friends he can play with in the afternoon?"

"No," answered Amina, with a tinge of exasperation and sadness. "I tell him not to leave the house. Two months ago, he tried to play with boys from those shacks. But they called him names. An old lady saved him before they beat him up. Thank God, I was home and I saw him running back. He looked like he was going to die. I calmed him down and told him, 'Don't play with those boys!'"

When she finished, she stiffened, clasped her mouth shut, and thrust her chin forward—the same posture of defiance the principal had seen earlier. It was as if she were saying, "We don't care. We can manage on our own."

The principal's face assumed a pensive, faraway look. He was convinced that, without help, the two orphans would face a hopeless and desolate existence. But with help, he believed, they would have a sporting chance at success. He began to realize that he had come without an adequate plan. Then after what seemed to be an interminable period of awkward silence, an idea occurred to him.

"Amina," the principal said, "it is very important for Ali to have at least two hours of playing time everyday. I will buy a ball and ask his classmates to play soccer every other day. Ali will have friends among his playmates and in the meantime have fun. I will start this project tomorrow. So, Ali, I want you to be at the school playground tomorrow, following the afternoon prayers. I shall be there."

Amina was not sure whether the principal's idea would make any difference. Ali had never bonded with his classmates and had never developed any real friendships among them. Besides, the traumatic experience with the neighborhood boys had left him distrustful of all except her and his teachers. She, however, knew that Ali had an itch for soccer—the very sight of children playing soccer excited him. What Amina couldn't foresee was whether Ali's classmates would accept him as a playmate.

Ali, on the other hand, was beset by the conflicting emotions of delight and fear.

Taking note of the changes in Ali's face, from jovial to somber and back again, the principal moved closer to him and smiled. But Ali still seemed confused.

Still smiling, the principal moved towards the door. Before leaving, he turned and gave Amina one more scrutinizing look. *What a courageous woman!* He thought. *If Ali ever beats the long odds against him, he will owe his success to his sister.* He waved goodbye. Amina waved back.

Amina and Ali sat down to their usual supper of hard bread and tea. After supper they chatted for a while and then retired for the night.

Ali always looked forward to nightfall because he preferred the dark to daylight. Daylight gave him an uneasy sense of exposure to a mysterious world he could not understand. The sight of groups and gatherings petrified him, because all seemed to know that he was a Yibir and an orphan. Daylight made him acutely cognizant of himself and his loneliness. Contrarily, in the dark he found cover and security from prying eyes, and he was not that distinct from his surroundings. It did not matter that his shorts were frayed, his shirt too small and patched up in too many places, and his hair infested with lice. The darker it was the better he felt.

He liked to sleep under an open window so he could look up and gaze at the stars, which had always fascinated him. There were so many of them, and they looked so beautiful. They were bright; they twinkled; and he could make out countless formations. They were also friendly, unlike the merciless sun. Stars had always been there in the past, and they would continue to be there in the future. Did they know where his father was? Did they know how his mother died? He would continue to watch and think and go from happy to sad and back until his eyelids felt heavy. He would then burrow under his cover sheet or under an old quilt when cold and gradually fall asleep.

Ali had recurring nightmares. The most frequent came in the form of an enormous monster. It would first appear in the distance and then move towards him, its large head swaying from side to side. Slowly but surely it would come closer and closer. Ali would boldly wait until he could see it clearly. The monster had the most grotesque shape imaginable. With bulging eyes, jutting canine teeth, spearlike claws and a large, spherical head, it was part human, part beast. Chilling screams emanated from its belly. "Run! Run!" a voice commanded, and Ali would try with all his might to run and scream at the same time. He would then wake up with a start only to find himself cradled in Amina's arms.

The night of the principal's visit, Ali eagerly went to his mat, filled with the anticipation of what the next day might bring. In the recent past, moments of yearning to play soccer had elicited torturous flashbacks from his traumatic experience with the neighborhood children. This time, though, he hoped things would be different because of the principal's involvement.

Running, jumping, and chasing a ball all afternoon would be quite thrilling. But how would he play soccer? He had seen other children playing the game, but he had never been able to join them. A tingling sensation ran through his feet as he imagined how it would feel when he actually kicked a ball. Surely his classmates had more soccer skills than he. He had a giddy but pleasant feeling in his chest, and he had difficulty sleeping. Then, as he had done so often in the past, he lay on his back, looked through the window, and gazed at the stars. *They look like illuminated balls,* he thought before he sank into a deep and peaceful sleep.

The principal came out and stepped into the dark moonless night. The sky was clear; the stars were very bright, and the air was nice and cool. But deep down inside, he was feeling unsettled. Frantz Fanon's *The Wretched of the Earth* came to his mind.

The two children already bore deeper and older scars (some handed down through generations) than he would ever know. And they would suffer more wounds to their psyche until they died. In the calendar of human ordeals, he was the child, not them. *How humbling!* he exclaimed to himself.

A stream of conflicting emotions grabbed him. On the one hand, he felt good for having spent time with Amina and Ali. On the other, he felt downhearted by his inability to help them in any significant way. And in this moment of utter aloneness, he could feel himself among a ghostly multitude marching slowly and singing "*We shall overcome*...."

Less than thirty yards from the squalid shacks, he stepped into a shallow pit and fell. He tried to get up by supporting himself with his right arm, but he lost his balance and fell backwards. A displeased donkey farted, snorted, and galloped away, braying loudly and angrily. As if on cue, a peel of feminine laughter came from the shacks. In his second attempt, the principal rose and walked more carefully, navigating his way through the bevy of shacks. Four women sitting in front of a hovel turned and craned their necks as he went by. He trudged on and crossed the playground. The memory of the school children he had seen playing soccer brought a smile to his face.

A short time later, he stepped into his favorite teashop and squinted to shield his eyes from the glare of the hissing lantern. Radio Hargeisa played Magool, Somalia's best female vocalist. He sat down, lit a Rothmans cigarette, and ordered tea. As he smoked and sipped the tea, he found himself unable to shake off the image of the two Yibirs. Leaning back on his wooden chair, he gradually surrendered himself to his thoughts.

We Africans, he lamented, *accuse the white man of bigotry, yet we practice the same intolerance with our own! When shall we learn?*

For a long time Yibirs had fascinated and intrigued him. Yes, based on Somali lore, Yibirs were at the bottom of the Somali caste system. But unlike Midgans and Tumals[4], who could gain approval by accepting their respective ranks and roles in society, Yibirs remained unwanted and unwelcome.

The principal silently reminisced about a Yibir he had known in his youth. Very dark and tall and strong, this Yibir had been endowed with a remarkable physique. In his twenties at the time, the Yibir tended a public garden and only occasionally ventured into the busy section of the town to buy supplies. Two things about the Yibir stood out in the principal's mind. The first was the image of the Yibir clad in a spotless white T-shirt and khaki shorts, carrying purchases in each hand, and walking away into the approaching night. Impassive, talking little, rarely smiling, head held high, neck and back straight, walking with a dignified air, he was an unfathomable but graceful sight.

The second was the unfortunate moment when the principal, as a young boy, admonished the Yibir, "Don't poison people!" and the Yibir complained to an adult relative of the principal, "What are we to be poisoning people?"

---

[4] Midgans and Tumals are among Somalia's subjugated and alienated minorities. Traditionally, Midgans have been skilled hunters, shoemakers and barbers; Tumals have been blacksmiths.

The principal now wished he could retract his stupid remark and undo the hurt he had inflicted on the hardworking Yibir.

"What is the matter with you? Finally in love?" the principal heard. With a weary face, he looked up to see three of the school's teachers standing over him. Feeling like he had woken up from a sad dream, he managed to smile and invited them to sit down and play cards.

Early the following morning, Ali was up and about and rearing to go. Unable to bate his excitement, he told some of his classmates about the plan before the principal had a chance to tell them. Towards the end of the school day, the principal walked into Ali's classroom and announced that, thenceforth, there would be soccer drills three times a week. Signing up would be voluntary, but those who did would have to show discipline. The principal asked those who wanted to join to raise their hands. Excitedly and cheerfully, the boys did—a testament to the dazzling allure the majestic sport of soccer held for boys in many parts of the world.

Soon Ali and his playmates were playing soccer with ebullient pleasure and a lot of kicking and racing for the ball without regard to spacing. They could be seen late in afternoons, running around en masse, abruptly changing direction like a school of fish dancing harmoniously in the sea. They could be heard in the distance, giggling and communicating in cheerful bursts of birdlike warbles.

Ali's introduction to soccer worked like a charm. He, naturally fast and agile, fell in love with the ball. He found it friendly and playful, and he saw no mystery around it. It favored no boy over another, and it was a delight to touch, to kick, and to chase. The bouncy ball, at once soft and hard, was like a playful hare. Catching it with the foot or the shin or the head was like a joyful kiss.

Within a few weeks, Ali's condition improved dramatically. His somber look gave way to glowing eyes; his indolence to cheerful vigor. The decline in his academic performance was reversed, just in time for him to rank third in his class in the final exam.

Chapter 3

Kinship with the Beasts

Ali's early years following his father's death were largely uneventful. He and Amina lived in indigence. But the care she provided, soccer, and school were sources of much comfort to him. Gradually, his life fell into an acceptable routine, except for one increasingly disturbing problem.

As he grew up, he crept slowly but steadily into the reality of being a Yibir. People of his kind were treated with disdain and the very word *Yibir* was an epithet. To be called a Yibir was to be insulted harshly. He wondered why and how Yibir differed from the names of other Somali clans. "If Yibir is such a vile word," he would ask himself, "why have my people taken it as a name?"

He talked, ate, laughed, played, sang, cried, slept, bled, grew, and looked like other children. He could see nothing different about himself. Yet, wherever he went, he felt he was seen as savage and stupid and base and unclean. The dark shame of his Yibirness followed him like a shadow. And he was made to feel that, somehow, it was his fault that he was a Yibir.

He was passive and peaceful. Sometimes he did find himself in situations that could lead to fights. But often someone would intervene and urge the opposing party to "leave the Yibir alone" or to "beware of the Yibir's eye!"

Such comments intrigued Ali as much as they hurt him. Did harm come to anyone who hurt a Yibir? Did this mean the Yibir was feared as much as he was despised? Ali did not know what to make of the conflicting messages.

He did continue to gambol and play soccer with his playmates. His ease with them, however, was limited to the schoolhouse and the soccer field. Outside of these two settings, his playmates were like strangers to him.

Then, one Friday morning, five of Ali's soccer companions invited him to join them to go hunting. Ali, thirteen years of age at the time, was of two minds about this invitation. On the one hand, he feared he might not fit in; on the other, he was eager for a day of youthful adventure. Going against the grain, he accepted.

Ali and five teammates met at a small farm owned by the family of one of the boys, Mohamed. Mohamed led out two dogs. Saeed, who had a knack for finding a dog or two, brought another. At midmorning, they moved out, heading north towards the woods. They walked briskly and in silence, like Pygmies hunting in the great forest of the Congo.

Soon Ali felt a clash of emotions. In him wrestled curiosity and fear. He was going away from home, away from school, away from the soccer field—his only comfort zones—and onto uncharted ground. He walked with trepidation, hiding his anxiety from his friends.

It was a sprightly April day, and the sun shone bright in a clear sky. The earth was soft and verdant, and the shrubs and acacia trees were in bloom. The twitter of the birds mingled with the piercing chirps of various insects coming back to life in the rainy season. Hither and thither a disturbed bird flew away or a frightened squirrel zipped by. The smell of spring filled the air. And the ubiquitous lepidoptera added color and danced vigorously, as if to celebrate the vernal joining of heaven and earth in a lawful union.

Looking around him, Ali began to calm down. Quiet and solitude comforted him. Away from home and outside of soccer, he had never felt in such harmony with his surroundings. And he, who had always been afraid of the unknown, now saw no mystery about the wilderness. It was as if the wilderness accepted him as kin. He blended into it seamlessly. The wilderness gave him a sense of levity and freedom and made his imagination soar. The near-total absence of any human hand touched him deeply and unleashed some hidden exhilarating power.

Barely thirty minutes into their walk, Adan turned to the rest and asked, "You heard what happened the night before last?"

The boys slowed down, some tittering, some raising their eyebrows. Adan was given to telling farfetched stories, though at times he was proven right.

"Faiza's older sister, Halwo, is in big trouble," whispered Adan, stretching his mouth sideways and wrinkling his cheeks.

"What sort of trouble?" asked Elmi, drawing closer to Adan and narrowing his eyes. "She is a modest girl."

"No, no. That isn't what I mean. The police commander has asked for her hand."

"Isn't that a good thing?" Mohamed interjected.

"You are missing the point. People think he is actually a Midgan!" Adan said, his eyes bulging as if he were high on *kat*[1]. To underscore the enormity of the story, he opened his hands and held his arms wide apart.

With piqued interest, the group formed a circle around Adan, who seemed more and more energized.

"He doesn't look like a Midgan though," protested Saeed, looking incredulous.

"Just listen to me, boys! The man could be a Midgan. I am not saying that he is a Midgan for sure. But he could be one. Anyway, Halwo's family is divided over the issue. Her father is too nice, and he has agreed, and Halwo herself loves the man. But all of her brothers and her uncle Omar, are dead set against marrying her off to a man they think is a Midgan. Actually her brothers have vowed to kill both Halwo and the police commander if the marriage takes place." Adan was now exasperated that the other boys did not seem to grasp the seriousness of the matter.

In apparent disgust, Saeed dismissed the whole story as not worth their while. "I shouldn't care even if he were a Yibir. She isn't my sister," He said, stressing the word Yibir.

"You are but a child. What do you know about such matters?" Adan countered, condescendingly.

Saeed became angry and made a few insulting remarks that made Adan angry. The two were about to fight. Adan was older and bigger, but Saeed was the more aggressive of the two. Before they came to blows, Mohamed and Dualeh intervened. They pleaded with Adan and Saeed to shake hands, which they did on the spot. Everybody laughed except

---

[1] The kat leaf is a mild stimulant favored by many Somalis.

Ali, who remained silent throughout the incident. Saeed's Yibir comment stuck in his craw and reopened a wound that had barely healed.

One cloudy afternoon, almost two weeks earlier, Ali had been walking home when he saw a boy hounding his sister. The boy was throwing rocks at her and calling her Yibir and other vile names. Amina was trying to run towards the house and dodge the rocks simultaneously. Adding insult to injury, Ali's appearance did not deter the boy who was older and bigger than he. But the boy's size was not enough to give Ali second thoughts. Enraged as he had never been, Ali charged.

Amina stopped and shouted, "Get to the house! Get to the house! Get away from him!"

Oblivious to his sister's pleas, Ali continued as if possessed. As he accelerated towards him, the offending boy froze in his tracks. Ali crashed into the boy. The boy fell on his back. Ali quickly got on top of the boy, took hold of his neck and began to strangle him. Horrified by what she saw, Amina ran towards the two boys. At the same time a crowd of people were rushing towards the two boys and shouting. Amina reached the boys first.

"Get off him! Get off him!" she screamed. But Ali either could not hear her or did not want to let go of the boy. The cacophony from the fast-approaching crowd might have drowned her voice. She grabbed Ali by the shoulders and pulled him. Then, to her chagrin, the other boy got on top of Ali. What could Amina do now? Nothing!

Too terrified to touch the offending boy, she waited for the crowd to arrive. When the crowd reached them, Amina cried and begged a man with fiery eyes to pull the boys apart. His pendent lower lip trembling, the fuming man started to talk but changed his mind and lunged forward to pull his son away.

"Shame on you!" the man shouted angrily at his son. "How can you degrade yourself so much and fight a Yibir? Yibirs are too timid, and they possess the evil eye. Beating a Yibir is no honor. Only a Yibir is fit to fight another Yibir!"

Grunts and growls punctuated the man's words, as he glared at Amina, who shook with fear. Amina understood the situation clearly

and knew that she and Ali were lucky. For both of them to escape serious bodily harm, Ali had to lose, which he did with her help. This was
what every adult Yibir knew and every Yibir child had to learn.

"Thank Allah!" said Amina, with a big sigh of relief as she held
Ali by the arm and led him away to the safety of home, sweet home.

Intimidated by the boy's enraged father, Ali had kept quiet at the
scene. But even in the safety of home, he did not question his sister.
He understood. And he was learning to submit meekly in the face of
Aji aggression. There was no chance for a Yibir victory over an Aji.

Now, thanks to Saeed's Yibir comment, the raw emotions of that
disturbing incident attacked Ali with a vengeance and put him out
of his element. He knew that he should not have come with the boys.
Their company had become a suffocating weight that limited his freedom and reminded him of who he was. His happiness, he felt, lay
apart from humanity. Humanity handicapped him severely and held
him in a kind of mental enslavement. He regarded the boys with
renewed suspicion and resentment and wished he could be alone.

After the near fight between Adan and Saeed, the pack moved
again. A short while later, they came upon a glade. Elmi broke into a
trot. Soon the rest joined him. It became a race. When they stopped,
Ali was last, to the surprise of all.

"I beat you all!" Elmi gloated.

"No, you didn't," Dualeh replied. "You just had a head start on us."

"Do you want to race me now?"

"Yes!"

"Just wait a minute, boys!" Mohamed interjected. "Let's all race,
and let it be fair this time."

"Okay, let's do it," Saeed seconded.

All the boys stood in line. Saeed started to count, "One, two…"
Then Elmi shouted, "First, I have to piss," and walked away to relieve
himself behind a tree.

Soon all the boys, except Ali, were urinating like an excited herd
of camels. Ali just waited, still and silent, at his position on the line.

He knew he could quite easily beat them all, and he wanted to show it this time. The group repositioned themselves on the line. But once again, there was an interruption, this time from garrulous Adan.

"I sprained an ankle two weeks ago," Adan claimed, stepping away from the line and limping slightly.

"Then, you count," Elmi said.

"Okay, I will," Adan replied and started, "One, two, three." At "three," the boys sprang forward and ran.

Ali responded late. *I will catch them*, he thought, *as I always do*. But his legs were too weak or too unwilling to carry him. He pushed and pushed and pushed, but to no avail. Then, as they closed in on the tree that marked the finish line, he felt his stomach and bowels sink and his limbs tighten, and he knew he was beaten. He was last. Mohamed won the race.

"Ali, you okay?" asked Dualeh, looking concerned.

"I feel fine," replied Ali, taking pains to hide his disappointment and confusion.

But the boys were puzzled, as they all knew there was only a ghost of a chance they could beat a healthy Ali.

The sun crawled higher and higher in the blue sky, and the shadows grew shorter and shorter. It was approaching lunchtime, but the boys felt as if they had not even started yet. They moved on farther.

Then all of a sudden, "Look!" shouted Elmi, pointing to a snake molt beside a rodent path.

"This molt is fresh, which means the snake is near," warned Elmi, looking around carefully.

The boys took a slight detour around the suspected area and silently scuttled. Shortly, they stumbled upon a large tortoise moving slowly and gracefully like a great grandfather. The hard, brown carapace glistened in the sun. Everyone stopped, crouched, and gazed. The small head retracted into the grand shell, and the baby-faced life turned into a hard stone. The boys marveled and laughed at the magnificent animal that was a symbol of mystery, sloth, age, peace, and patience. They toyed with it for a while, trying to coax it out of its shell. The three dogs jumped back and forth around the intriguing rock, sniffing, barking, and wagging their tails.

Ali's eyes lingered on the splendid shell. A wisp of peace of mind blew on him. *A wall! A wall! A protective wall!*

Left alone, the tortoise proceeded with its long, plodding and persistent journey through life and time.

They climbed and stood on top of a hillock. The air was clear and calm, and they could look and see far and wide. In the distance, they could see the town—a beautiful panoptic view of neatly ordered one-story row houses. A carpet of green grass dominated the surrounding landscape. The town stood as a solid center, a focus, and a unifying force for the mountain range and the woods to the north and the plains to the south, east and west. The scene exerted a vaguely pleasant pull on the boys. They studied the view and pointed out salient features: the main streets, the post office, the police station, the school, the main mosque, the Court of Justice, the playground, and the Garden of Liberty.

"Splendid!" Dualeh exclaimed. The other boys agreed with him.

Their eyes traveled to the shantytown. A dull structure of light brown dried mud, the shantytown lay like a faceless corpse. A short distance to the east of the mangy shacks, a few animals grazed. The boys' eyes moved out and farther and settled on an isolated hut standing like a condemned man facing the firing squad. In silence and one by one, the boys looked at Ali—who stood impassive, feeling dull and sick—and turned away, as if suddenly reminded of who he was.

They descended the hillock and sat under a shady tree to rest. A minute or two later, restless Elmi jumped to his feet and clambered the acacia tree. Sitting on a thick bough, he sang a popular song. In the middle of the song, he abruptly stopped and moved to another bough. Soon the rest of the boys could see his target: shimmering lumps of gum with thin strands shaped like dripping honey. Elmi grabbed the chunks of gum, put one in his mouth and dropped the rest down to his friends. Then he shinnied down the tree, as they all sucked and munched on the gum.

Not done yet, Elmi faced away from the other boys, who watched him closely and with interest. A comedian and a prankster, he had the boys wondering what he had up his sleeve this time. Shortly, he faced them, pretending to be reading from notes. He talked softly and demurely and threw occasional suspicious glances at "his students." From time to time, he locked eyes with one of the boys. Then, feigning offense, he looked down only to look up again, to see if the "offender" was still staring at him. All the boys laughed as they recognized the person he was imitating: a teacher who, though diligent and conscientious, resented being looked at squarely in the eye.

Elmi signaled a new act. He walked into the "classroom," adjusting his glasses. "Today," he announced, in a crisp, lively voice, "we will discuss some concepts of geometry. It is simple." His rapidly shifting eyes crisscrossed the "classroom." The boys knew which teacher Elmi was mimicking now and they listened and watched joyfully. A highly lovable teacher, the subject of impersonation was as famous for his brisk gestures when explaining difficult concepts as he was for his "We will add just a little bit" trademark phrase.

"Let's go," Mohamed said, with a sense of urgency.

The boys rose to their feet. Suddenly, a rabbit leapt from under a clump of tall grass and darted speedily across the field.

"Catch it!" the boys shouted to the dogs.

The three dogs sped after the rabbit, now well ahead of them. The boys fanned out, forming a wide line, and ran to surround the rabbit's intended refuge: a thicket in the distance. Meanwhile, one of the dogs was closing in on the rabbit. The gray rabbit glided through the air and through the grass and bounced on the soft and moist ground. Soon its rapidly flicking hind legs were almost within a striking distance of the powerful paws of the fast-approaching dog. The brown dog huffed and puffed and surged ahead punishing the tender grass and flinging clods of earth as it did so. But then the rabbit swerved sharply, causing the dog to skid awkwardly. By the time the dog recovered, the rabbit was far away and beyond reach.

The boys came together and stopped to catch their breath. The dogs stood and panted heavily, lolling their tongues and shifting their eyes rapidly, all in a vain attempt to blame the boys for their defeat.

"Rabbits will only get us and the dogs tired," Dualeh said. "Let's look for warthogs instead."

"But we caught rabbits before. I say let's catch whatever we can find," Mohamed objected, sounding irritated and impatient.

The other boys agreed with Mohamed. In the end, whatever they could kill would be food for the dogs. So why would they look for a particular type of game?

Hungry for a kill, the boys and the dogs moved with the zest of hunters after redemption. They walked up an acclivity and surveyed the surroundings.

"A warthog!" shouted Saeed.

It was indeed a warthog—its prognathous head hanging down, its muzzle almost touching the ground, its short spiny tail upright like an antenna.

The boys ran down the slope and scudded stealthily until they came within about sixty yards of the animal. The warthog stopped, and raised its head, as if to sniff or to see more clearly. It was surrounded! Rocks and short clubs at the ready, the boys stood quiet, attentive and nervous. The dogs, their muzzles jerking up and down, barked menacingly and joined the boys in an intense moment of indecision.

The warthog paced back and forth, as if to take stock. Then it suddenly charged, galloping and reaching top speed in but several leaps. Not even a fool would stand in the way of a charging warthog. Dropping their clubs and their rocks, the boys took to their heels. And, in a just turn of fate, the hunter and the hunted exchanged roles.

Unable to get out of the way fast enough, Adan was caught. But not even he could tell how. All anyone could later remember was a briefly airborne Adan, and the warthog either slipping under him or running over him. No one pursued the warthog. Instead, the boys raced to Adan, who rose to his feet and fell several times, all the while screaming, "I broke a leg! No, I didn't! I broke a leg! No, I didn't!"

It took the boys a while to see that, except for bruises on his hands, elbows, and knees, Adan was unscathed. They laughed and made fun of the incident and, far from returning home, pressed forward for more adventure.

Around noon, the boys felt thirsty and decided to turn to a pond about half a mile away. They knew the pond would be almost full because it had rained heavily the week before. They covered the distance in a slow trot.

At the pond, they found a group of maids washing clothes. Here and there, garments, some white and spotless, others brightly florid, lay spread out on rocks to dry. Some of the girls were squatting by their wash tubs and moving their hands vigorously under thick, white foam. Others were rinsing clothes, wringing them, and laying them out. One girl was plaiting another's hair and singing a country song. Bubbles, large and small, glided in the air and carried with them the smell of washing powder. Fresh floral scents wafted over the water.

The boys had often fantasized about meeting girls and talking to them. But now that they were face to face with them—in a secluded area, far and free from the watchful eyes of chaperones—their loquacious tongues froze and waxed silent. Their amorous hearts pumping faster and harder in a fit of nervousness, they threw small rocks into the water. They listened to the splashes and watched the rocks sink. And they watched small waves spread and ripple out smoothly to the edges of the pond. Meanwhile, the girls whispered among themselves, and threw short and furtive glances at the boys and smiled at them invitingly. But the boys, unable to rise to the occasion, merely drank their fills and slunk away.

About a hundred yards later, the boys, walking silent and embarrassed by their confused state of mind at the pond, stumbled upon another rabbit cowering under a clump of tall grass. With a brisk and giant leap, the rabbit bolted. Adan hurled a short club forcefully. The hurtling club and the speeding rabbit collided. The crushed rabbit attempted to rise and bolt again; but it was in vain. On the ground the rabbit lay, back grotesquely disjoined, hind legs limp and lifeless, ears erect and slanted back.

The tiny rabbit strove mightily. The neck twitched and jerked up and down. And the front legs kicked and pawed and clawed in a desperate attempt to cling to life. But then, the dogs ripped off chunks of flesh and bone. A few minutes later, only blotches of blood and bits of bone and a lifeless head remained of the once bouncy rabbit. One eye stared blankly into space; the other had given way to a deep and bloody hole.

Ali's heart froze from guilt and horror. To him, it looked as if the pawing was a plea for help from the dying animal. But he had no control over the course of events.

The hunters cleared the woods and were now in a grassy field, not far from the airstrip where a plane from Aden[2] landed once a week. And, there, the boys spotted a warthog and her farrow trotting in the direction of the woodland. Led by the dogs, the boys ran. When the warthog spotted the dogs and the boys, she turned back and trotted faster, her brood running in a single file behind her. The boys, running at top speed, formed a phalanx to cut the warthogs off before they reached their lair.

The moment Ali saw the little piglets and their mother in flight for their lives, an eerie feeling came over him. The scene, he felt, spelled doom and disaster. Too unnerved to run fast, he dragged his leaden feet (first one, then the other) his eyes fixed on the tiny beasts.

The boys and the dogs closed in. The mother must have realized they were not going to make it home, as their lair was quite a distance away. They reached an unfinished hole before the boys and the dogs could intercept them. Then the mother herded the five little piglets into the hole and scrambled in after them.

When the boys reached the hole, they saw it was shallow. Only a few feet below ground, the large head of the mother covered the hole like a solid rock. Something about the mother's blinking eyes grabbed Ali's attention and held him spellbound. But the other boys and the dogs were delighted. A huge sow and five little piglets all so close and in such a small hole! Only the ominously long and curved tusks of

---

[2] The capital city of what was then South Yemen, across the Red Sea from Somalia.

the mother stood in the way.

The dogs barked and jumped back and forth in front of the hole. Now and then, the sow lunged forward and shoveled a large scoop of earth into the faces of the dogs and the boys, who scampered away and then quickly returned. The standoff continued, all the while the five little piglets staying soundly tucked away behind their mother.

Lulled into a false sense of safety, one of the dogs stepped down into the den. Then the mother suddenly lunged forth to dig its tusks into the enemy. It was too late for the foolish dog to jump back to dodge the blow. The sow's advancing tusks and the dog's receding abdomen came in contact. A heavy grunt and a whimper could be heard, and the dog was rudely repulsed partly by the blow and partly by its instinctive attempt to evade the blow. Once out of the hole, the dog eased itself to the ground and licked a gaping wound. Fortunately, the wound was superficial, and a few minutes later the dog rose and walked, first gingerly, then normally. This was the second casualty the hunting team had suffered, the first being Adan, who was now standing quite a distance away from the fray.

The stalemate continued, the boys and the dogs keeping a safe distance away from the raging warthog. All the mother had to do was wait and wait and wait, until the boys gave up and turned back. The incident would have been only a crude but important lesson of survival for the five little piglets. But without any urgent cause, the sow bolted with quick giant leaps. The boys and the dogs scattered and ran in fright. But it was only the sow's final half-hearted show of force. When she saw the way was clear, she galloped away.

The sudden change in the piglets' fortune jolted Ali. All day, he had felt strangely torpid and disgusted by the boys' wanton violence. In him swelled an uncanny sense of kinship with the hunted animals. The lot of the ill-fated rabbit haunted him. The sad specter of the warthog galloping away—and leaving her five little piglets cowering in the shallow hole—jarred him deeply. But the worst, he knew, was still to come. And all he could do was watch with a vexed mind and a mournful heart.

It was like shooting fish in a barrel. The dogs went in with a vengeance to fish the piglets out one at a time, as if to prolong a sweet sport. Too young to have grown tusks and large butting heads, the piglets looked tender and beautiful. They came out squealing and vainly tried to outrun the dogs. But their short and frail legs failed them. They ran in jumbled circles and squealed without pause. And they sought refuge around the feet of the boys whose legs must, to them, have appeared like tree trunks. The boys cleared the way for the dogs to operate unobstructed and with impunity. Some even kicked the little piglets so that the dogs could get to them more easily. The plump and small piglets fell on their sides but bounced up quickly and repeatedly tried to hide behind the boys.

The boys reveled in the sight of vengeful dogs burying their sharp canines into the yielding bodies of the piglets. But the scene made Ali's flesh crawl. Every stab into the piglets felt like a stab into his heart; and every squeal felt as if it emanated from deep inside him. Squatting a distance away, he watched, dazed and distressed.

Gradually, and after much agony, the squeals stopped one by one. The last little piglet went into the convulsions of death and stopped kicking with its tiny legs. Then the euphoric boys and the triumphant and feasted dogs left the blood-spattered scene. Ali brought up the rear, slogging like a wounded animal.

It was already well past noon, and the boys were hungry and thirsty. They decided to turn towards a nearby farmhouse and ask for water. The farm was a large, fenced field covered with tall, green grass. The field was adorned with a few scattered trees, fifteen cows and one large ox— which was conspicuous by its hump and domed horns. The colorful skins of the cattle shimmered under the bright sun. Some of the cows dozed; others grazed lazily and swished their long hairy tails against their sides. The ox eyed the boys and the dogs haughtily then, deeming them of no import, looked away. A large hut stood outside the walled field. Next to the hut was a deep man-made well. To complete the bucolic scene, a young girl of about fifteen with braided hair stood just outside the hut. As she saw the boys and the dogs, her lower jaw dropped a little; and her eyes opened wider and shone brighter. City boys!

"*Assalamu alaikum*[3]!" Mohamed greeted.

"*Wa alaikuma assalam*[4]!" she replied, her hand reaching to her uncovered head and running smoothly over the braids.

She stepped back and murmured through the door, which she held ajar. An old man with a silvery beard emerged and stood in the doorway. Squinting, he raised his right hand to shield his eyes against the sun and greeted the boys. Then he spoke to the girl in a low voice, addressing her as his granddaughter. She took out mats and laid them out under a tree. And she fetched a large pot of milk and an enameled mug.

"Uncle, you don't have to do this," Mohamed protested. "We want only water."

"You are young men. You need to fill your stomachs with milk, not water," replied the old man, wagging his finger.

The old man filled the mug and handed it to Elmi, the youngest looking. Elmi, in conformity to tradition, offered it to each of the other boys, starting with the one sitting next to him. They all bid Elmi drink the milk. He drank as much as he could. And so it went, each time the old man making sure the cup was full to the brim.

"Now, tell me who you are," the old man asked. He wanted to know the full names of the boys and their respective clans.

One by one, they told him who they were.

"Your grandfather died in my arms in Burma, where we fought the Japanese. No braver man has ever been born of a Somali mother. He...he was killed by a sniper," he said, a little pensively, to one of the boys.

Then it was Ali's turn to say who he was. But how could he identify himself? Had he told the old man he was a Yibir, the old man would have seen him as a lowlife among thoroughbreds. Never had Ali felt so far removed from Aji boys. Under the old man's penetrating eyes, he wilted and became an individual of no significance. His personality evaporated into a state of nothingness. His lower jaw fell, and he gave the old man a wide-eyed look of incredulity.

---

[3] May peace be upon you.
[4] May peace be upon you, too.

"I understand," said the old man, abandoning the subject. Ali's chagrin and his humble bearing said it all.

The old man asked the boys to stay longer so that he could give them tea. But the boys refused and stood up to shake hands with him and left.

Dejected and oblivious of the boys' joyous and boisterous chatter about the day's events, Ali trudged slowly behind the pack. A few minutes later, he stopped and looked back. High in the sky, vultures circled above the spot where, a little more than an hour earlier, five little piglets had met their brutal fate. Shuddering a little and laying his hand on his breast, he felt his heart's sluggish beating in his frail and hollow chest. An owl hooted mournfully as he walked home alone and lonely.

It was almost dark when he reached home. Amina was sitting outside waiting for him to arrive. As he approached, she could see the dreary and fatigued look on his face. He passed her without a word. She watched him intensely and thoughtfully, then shook her head. *Not yet*, she thought. *Not yet!*

In the days that followed, Ali's mistrust of people grew. Everywhere he went— except for school, the playground, and home— he felt naked and threatened. And he could think of no way to draw a veil over his nakedness. He was different from his playmates. They were cruel and ruthless; he was sensitive. And their cruelty to the animals reminded him of the day the neighborhood boys hounded him and chased him. He identified more with the victims—the slaughtered rabbit and the little piglets—than he did with the victimizers. Vivid images from the hunting venture haunted him and stirred sharp twinges of guilt in him. And he grew more compassionate to animals and now looked differently upon the donkeys and the stray dogs and cats, which other children his age liked to tease, stone, and chase. Inasmuch as the noble Ajis were brutal, Ali felt he was in league with the beasts.

Chapter 4

Dreams in the Spring of Life

Hope springs eternal.
— Alexander Pope

Ali grew increasingly more timid and more likely to follow others than to lead them. Yet shyness and subservience brought him neither acceptance nor respect. He faced the daunting realization that he was still an undesirable. So he distanced himself from all except his sister. And he concentrated his emotional energy on the two endeavors he found rewarding: soccer and school. Soccer entertained him and gave him a semblance of acceptance and attention. School gave him a fair ground on which to compete, excel, and triumph over his more fortunate coevals.

In the summer of the year after the hunting venture, Ali had little to do except play soccer in the afternoons. Having long decided to confine his association with his playmates to the playground, he had long idle hours. This situation raised the principal's concern that Ali might relapse into a state of depression. So he got Ali a job as a waiter in the town's classiest café. Ali would work the afternoon shift, from four to ten in the evening, when the elite of the town frequented the place. He would earn sixty shillings[5] a month plus one meal a day and have Fridays off. He was fourteen years old.

Ali was apprehensive. He would have to meet and mingle with people—lots of people—outside his comfort zone. He was reluctant to accept because he knew he would feel uneasy and insecure. But the principal prevailed upon him.

Ali soon found the café's owner pleasant to work with. In a matter of a few days, he found himself relatively comfortable. What is more,

[5] The equivalent of U.S. $10

earning money thrilled him. He waited with excitement for the time when, at the end of each month, he handed his full pay over to his sister. The first time he handed her the sixty shillings was one of the happiest of his life. Sure, Amina had often come up with enough money to buy him a new shirt, a new pair of pants, or a new pair of shoes for the Eid fiesta marking the end of the holy month of Ramadan. He, however, knew that Amina had to work hard and long hours for the money she earned. She needed help, and he was glad to do so.

Yet the significance of Ali's life as a waiter lay not in material gain. Rather it was the type of people he met and what he learned from them that would form a defining period in his life.

Among the customers of the café were a group of men who had received their college education in the United States. Initially, the way the men looked, sounded, and behaved was foreign to Ali. They seemed so remote from him even when he stood so close to them—pretentious men speaking in foreign tongues, mysterious men! So he did not pay them any particular attention. He just concentrated on his job, serving the customers and staying within earshot of them to take their orders. Gradually, however, he found these educated men from America interesting.

The group was quite an attraction. Often joined by government officials, businessmen, and teachers, they thrived as the center of attention, a position they strove to maintain. They spoke English as well as they spoke Somali, and did it with aplomb and flair. And they talked about intriguing things. It was not long before Ali began to look forward to the arrival of the group at the café and the sophisticated discussions that followed. Sitting a few yards from them and ready to take their orders, he would listen and enjoy their conversations. It did not matter that he did not understand a large part of what they talked about. Particularly fascinating to him was their ability to speak English fluently and effortlessly.

Ali liked the stories the foreign-educated men recounted about experiences they had had abroad. He was thrilled to hear of a world vastly different from his own—trains, bridges, cars, highways, planes, airports, ships, harbors, New York's skyscrapers. The numerous references to great thinkers and men and women of science left him awestruck. But what, more than anything else, cast a magic spell over him was talk of the universities, the professors, the libraries filled with books, and the science laboratories.

Ali was impatient for the days he would spend at the café, when he would mingle with the town's intellectual elite. And the intellectuals treated him well and told him that if he continued to do well at school he would have a good chance of being sent to America. It felt good to envision a glowing future, and it felt nice to be embraced by this elite group. The men became his role models, and what is more, he liked them.

For the first time in his young life, he dared to look far ahead into the future. By his second summer at the café, he was filled with vivid dreams. On one particular day, as he was headed home from work, he lost himself in a profoundly poignant reverie.

He was in America, attending a university and studying medicine. Everything was grand, and the people were nice, and he was doing well. Yes, he would write to his sister, and he would write often, and he would tell her about all the wonderful and exciting experiences he was having and living. Maybe he would decide to stay in America, as others had done. Then he would find a way to send for Amina. And they would live together, and he would do all the work and let her rest.

But, then, he remembered his father, and a wave of sadness swept over him. *I wish my father could be with us,* he lamented. *I would take care of him too, and we would be one very happy family.*

He reached home and found Amina awake, waiting for him.

"You know what, when I finish high school, I will go to America and study medicine!"

"How do you know? Somebody told you?" asked Amina, rising to her feet, taking a step towards him and holding her arms akimbo.

"No. I just know it. I feel it. The best students are sent to America and Britain for college education. There is no reason why I can't get it."

Amina squinted to study his face in the weak light of the kerosene lamp. He was in an unusual state of levity.

"First, finish high school," she cautioned.

"Of that there is no doubt. And I'll do very well too. Then I'll be sent to America."

"I will be happy enough if they let you be a clerk."

"Don't be pessimistic! The educated men I meet at the café tell me it is a sure thing. I shall go to America, and I shall be a doctor, and I shall take good care of you. We shall both be married, and I shall take care of all of our children. We shall be happy."

Amina was amused. A smile crept over her face. "One step at a time," she advised.

"I can feel and see and smell and touch the future! It is only a matter of time. Only a matter of time."

"If they will only let you," responded Amina, in a subdued but firm voice. Ali was far too excited though to pay attention to Amina's last comment on the subject.

For the first time in his life, he had a solid dream. The invigorating winds of hope blew and lifted him up, high, enabling him to endure the daunting present. By the end of his third and final summer as a waiter in the café, Ali was far from the moping, timid boy he had been. Before him lay two worlds: a depressing world that held him down as inferior and an inspiring world that held promise. One world troubled him and promised him an empty, unfulfilling, and tormented life. The other excited him with its universities and professors and science and books, all of which could make him great. He wanted to be part of this latter world— so bright and so fulfilling. He wanted to conduct and present himself accordingly. He wanted to banish that other dispiriting world from his mind.

It was to this upbeat and forward-looking Ali that Amina passed a message one dull September day.

"You remember Shukri, the lady who helped me find the job?" she asked.

"Yes," Ali replied.

"She wants you to tutor her daughter, the one that is graduating from intermediate school this year. She is concerned about her daughter's weakness in math. Can you help?"

"I shouldn't hesitate to help someone who has helped us. Ask her to tell us when and where. I can give her only about two hours a night, two nights of the week. I've got to study harder this year too." He was in his second year of high school.

"I'll let them know. By the way, the girl's name is Anissa. She only recently moved from Mogadishu, where she lived with her aunt."

For a week, Ali did not give much thought to the matter. Then Amina raised the subject again.

"You studying tonight?" she asked.

"You need me for something?"

"If you are not studying. I want to take you to the house of Abdalla's family. Abdalla is Shukri's husband and Anissa's father."

"Well, we can do that," Ali replied, nonchalantly.

"We will go tonight, after sunset prayers. We will meet here and then go straight to their house. Don't forget."

At about four o'clock in the afternoon, Ali put on a pair of dirty, old sneakers, a pair of shorts, and a faded but durable T-shirt, then headed for the playing field.

There were not enough boys on the field to constitute two complete teams. Therefore, they played three-on-three at a gentle pace. When he broke a sweat, he walked back home and splashed water over his body.

Amina gave him a hard loaf of kidar and a cup of tea. The combination of the hard bread and the tea tasted sweet. When he finished eating, he praised Allah for the hard baked dough and the tea and Amina and everything in life that he had. Then the brother and sister walked out together in silence.

Barely fifteen minutes later, they reached the house. Amina knocked on the door.

"Who is it?" a female voice asked.

"This is Amina. I have brought Ali with me."

Several moments later, the door was thrown open. Standing behind Amina, Ali could not at first see the person who had just opened the door.

A young woman's voice invited them to "come in." Amina went in first. Only then could Ali see a decorously covered young woman. He hesitated to enter. He could tell she was short and buxom. A wisp of very dark and silky hair showed on her partly covered face.

"Come in," repeated Anissa, motioning him to an inner room.

Ali strode inside awkwardly and entered the room, where Amina sat ensconced in a cushioned armchair. Facing Amina and sitting in another armchair was Anissa's mother. Ali sat next to his sister and found it surprisingly easy to look at the woman with the motherly face.

Amina and Shukri chatted and laughed, and it was a while before they turned to the issue at hand.

"I hear you are as good in soccer as you are in school. That is good!" Shukri complimented Ali.

From the look in her eyes, Ali could tell she was honest. Not knowing how to respond to the compliment, he could only offer a stiff smile. Shukri gave him one serious look, as if to size him up. Her face broke into an even bigger smile than before.

"How fast he has grown!" exclaimed Shukri. "It seems that it was only yesterday when he was but a frail child. By the grace of Allah, he has grown into a man!"

Looking at her brother with satisfaction and pride, Amina pursed her lips. Then, her eyes sparkling, she said, "It is all Allah's doing. Thanks and praise be due to Him."

At that very moment, Anissa walked in, holding a tray with three glasses of a cool soft drink—which, Ali later learned, was called Tang. Never had he tasted a drink so delicious.

"This is the girl I want you to tutor," Shukri introduced her daughter. "Her name is Anissa."

Anissa looked at her mother before she threw Ali a half-hearted glance. She then blushed a little and quickly looked away. Ali gave her a good look —as much a look as a boy could give to a girl under her mother's watchful eyes. She had a short, pointed nose and a small, diamond-shaped mouth. Her cheeks looked luscious, and her eyes glistened with life.

"Can you start tonight?" asked Shukri, looking from Ali to Amina and back.

"Yes, I am ready," Ali replied, only to feel immediate embarrassment that he had said so. He took his glass and emptied it.

"Let me refill it," said Anissa as she rose.

"No!" he protested—not willing to be seen as too eager for another glass, though he felt like drinking ten.

Shukri suggested that she and Amina move to another room. Ali and Anissa were left alone. Anissa fetched a notebook and a textbook—the first of a three-volume mathematics text published in Britain and, at the time, widely used among northern Somali students at the intermediate level. Ali had never owned a copy of any of the volumes. Yet he had solved almost every problem in them, because others who could afford to buy them had to seek his help.

"Show me the chapter you're working on," said Ali.

She showed him, and he suggested they do several problems together. He soon realized they would have to start from chapter one, and he told her so.

"The hard part is overcoming your fear of math and believing in your ability," Ali explained, emphasizing the word *ability*. "Believe me. I have learnt from the best. Do you remember the tall, lanky teacher with glasses who used to teach in the intermediate school?"

"No, I don't," replied Anissa, "I was away from Las Burgabo for six years. I lived with my aunt in Mogadishu[6]."

Ali shrugged and shook his head in a display of wonderment.

"What a great math teacher he was! Let me tell you a story. In our class, we had a student who was superior in languages but very poor in math. He flaunted and poked fun at his own weakness in math. But this teacher didn't want to give up on this guy. One day, he drew a rectangle on the board and marked the lengths of its sides. Then he

[6] Somalia's capital city

58

asked the student what the perimeter of the rectangle was. The student shook his head, I don't know. The teacher asked him the meaning of the word *perimeter*. 'All the way around,' answered the student. The teacher asked the student what the distance all the way around the rectangle was. But still the student couldn't tell. 'What does all the way around mean?' asked the teacher. 'The path along all the sides,' the student replied. 'What is the length of that path?' asked the teacher. 'The lengths of all the sides put together,' answered the student. 'Put them together,' the teacher barked, and the boy was able to give the answer. Within a year, that boy was one of the best math students in the school."

So began Ali's work to make Anissa a good math student. She did not become one of the best in the school; but, within a few months, her mathematical abilities improved significantly. Nine months later, she did well on the math section of the final exam, and her mother was elated and grateful to Ali. Unbeknownst to the mother, however, something else was happening at the same time.

From the beginning, Ali was very much impressed with Anissa's striking beauty; her charm, vitality, and maturity. Whenever she looked at him, an angelic smile graced her lively face. He felt that she respected him not only as a tutor but, more important, as a person. They exchanged stories, and she told him about her experiences in Mogadishu, which was much bigger than their town.

Initially, he was nervous in her presence. But her demeanor and conduct towards him won him over and calmed him down. It did not take him long to realize that he drew comfort from her. Gradually, the comfort changed to pleasure. Her company filled a void in his life—a void he had not known existed. Her gait, her look, her smile, and her soft but lively feminine voice titillated the insides of his chest and his abdomen. Even his teeth itched.

Within a few weeks, Anissa was on Ali's mind most of the time. Wherever he was, he felt pulled towards her, or towards where he thought she was. It was not just her beauty that attracted him. It was the way she walked, the way she talked, and even the way she sat. He would give her a problem to solve then lean back on his chair and watch. She would then tilt her head a little, rest it gently on her left hand, hold the pen in her right hand, and gracefully apply herself to the problem. If the problem was hard, she would raise her head slightly, eye him askance, pucker her face a little to feign annoyance, and go back to the problem with more verve and focus. He adored her and treated her gently and with care, as if she were as fragile and as fine as splendid china. The experience gave him sweet dreams of her at night— unlike the lusty, wet dreams he had of women he had barely known. The tingling sensations she stirred in him never reached below the waist. With her, there was only love, pure and simple.

Initially, he did not know if the feeling was mutual. Then he saw subtle but unmistakable signs. Her smiles lingered longer. Her eyes, sometimes half-closed, betrayed a lonely feeling. What had been a short, mirthful look, became a blissful gaze that rested softly on his eyes, then moved to his hair, his cheeks, his jaws, his mouth, down his neck to his shoulders and his chest, then back to his eyes again before it ended with a slight twitch of the corners of her mouth. It was pure and honest and mutual love, intensified many times over by their inability to talk about it and say, "I love you," to each other. It was a powerful force they felt and lived but did not quite know how to tend or groom.

Henceforth an integral part of his joyful dreams, Anissia provided him with a tenderness and a calm he had barely known. She might even join him in America, and they might study together. They would get married, and in the afternoons take strolls in the parks and streets he had heard so much about. Ah! These were moments of sublime imagination, when Ali's restless soul could find calm repose and love and hope.

Chapter 5

Back to Earth

Then one night, almost a year after he and Anissa first met, Ali decided to pay her a visit. The tutoring had come to an end when she had passed the dreaded final exam. She was now in the secondary school, two years behind Ali. But Ali continued, now and then, to show up at her home.

At about eight o'clock in the evening, he knocked on the door. There was no response. He knocked again. The door opened and revealed Anissa's cloaked figure looking down and sideways. A chill shot through Ali's entire body. Something was wrong, and he could sense it in his bones. She turned towards him. Their eyes met, and he could tell she had been crying. Smiling sheepishly, she raised her right hand as if to touch his hand. But when their hands met, she slipped him a roll of paper. Her hand trembled. Looking down to avoid his eyes, she opened the door and stepped aside. He understood it to mean good night. He turned away, took five steps, paused and then looked back towards her. She was still standing there, facing him. He blew her a kiss, something he had never done before. She did the same. And with this innocent and pained gesture he walked into the doleful night.

When he reached home, Amina was fast asleep. He sat by the kerosene lamp to unfold the paper. It was a brief letter written in Somali:

Dear Ali,

My father has given me away to a man who is a total stranger to me. I have been told that he is in his sixties and that he lives and works in Saudi Arabia. I now have the courage to say to you something I have never said to you before: I love you. I do not care about the customs that stand in our way. I will flee with you and marry you and live with you as long as I possess a beating heart, but only if you so desire. Do you have the will? Do you have the heart? Can you be a man and elope with me?

Anissa

What a sinking feeling! Had she said that she could not and would not ever see him again, he could have taken the hit. After all, he knew that the whole town would have been up in arms against a marriage between him and her. But this was something he could not have foreseen and was, thus, unprepared for. He read the letter again and again; and each time his heart filled with more and more pain. He wanted to cry, but he had forgotten how to cry. The rivers of tears flowed the other way and filled his veins. Ignoring his supper, he continued to sit by the lamp—his legs crossed, his head buried in his hands—until it was past midnight. Then he rose on weak and shaky legs, moved to his mat, and lay down with all his clothes on.

When Amina woke up for morning prayers, she saw her brother fast asleep, in his shoes and his clothing. She also found Ali's untouched supper of the night before. This odd and unseemly sight disturbed her. After her morning prayers, she made and drank a cup of tea. Next, she put the kettle and a cup beside a plate containing three pieces of *lahoh*[7] she had made at work the day before. At five-thirty in the morning, it was still too early to wake Ali. She took one more look at him, grimaced, and shook her head. Then she left for work.

Every morning except Fridays Amina arrived at Sahra's house early, to prepare breakfast for Sahra and her children. On this particular morning, she arrived earlier than usual and set to work. She made enough tea to fill a large thermos, then put flour into a bowl, mixed it with water and kneaded the resulting large mass of dough. She divided the dough into ten rolls and put them, one at a time, on a wooden board. Then she rolled them out with a rolling pin. Next, she took a pan and placed it on the *girgireh*[8], and poured a little oil in it. Then she gently spread the sheets of dough on the pan one at a time and baked them.

By the time the children had woken up, the aroma of Somali *kibis*[9] had pervaded the whole house. Amina asked each of the children and

---

[7] Very thin and very wide pancake, cherished in Somalia and Ethiopia
[8] Homemade stove
[9] Somali bread akin to, but thicker than, Indian Paratha

their mother what they wanted on the kibis: honey or sugar. She served the delicious, chewy bread and tea to all, including herself.

At nine o'clock in the morning, Amina—having washed the dishes and cleaned the house and made the beds—grabbed a basket and a twenty-shilling bill and set off for the market. She bought two liters of milk and three pounds of meat, along with onions, potatoes, tomatoes, and a head of cabbage. When she returned, she prepared dinner and waited for the children and their mother to arrive. Lately, she had been taking this window of time to teach herself how to read and write Somali.

By half past one in the afternoon, the family was back, and it was time for Amina to grab a small bowl of food and head home. Sahra would serve herself and her children, and Amina would serve Ali.

When she reached home, she found her brother crestfallen. He gave himself a violent shake of the head and feigned a smile. Amina, however, could see through this hollow, joyless smile. She served dinner without uttering a single word. Ali waited for her to talk, but for about half an hour neither said a word.

Then, finally, Amina asked, "What is the matter with you?" in a low but firm voice. She looked at him intensely, her face stern, lips pursed tight, jaws clasped.

He looked at her in a sad but relaxed manner. Then he put his right hand in the right pocket of his pants and pulled out Anissa's crumbled letter. She reached for the paper and held it delicately. *How could such a tiny, crumbled paper be so forceful as to cause Ali such anguish?*

With a tremulous hand, she unfolded the paper ball and looked at it. Reading the Somali words loomed as a challenge. But she had the will, and she took her time. Letter by letter, word by word, the formidable sentences came together and poured out the secret.

"You must forget about her!" Amina commanded, with the slightest change in her facial expression.

"You read it!" Ali shouted.

"Yes!" she responded. A triumphant smile showed on her face. In this moment of uncertainty and anguish, the significance of her ability to read was not lost on either of them. But the celebration was brief. In a minute, her face turned serious again.

"You must forget about her!" she repeated.

Amina had always thought Ali's interest in Anissa was mere infatuation, which would blow over in time. Though approaching thirty, she was unsophisticated in matters of the heart. How could she understand, when every sprouting romance she had ever had perished under the weight of her grievous life? With her, romance was never more than a flicker in the eyes and a momentary thrill that swept through her like a warm, delectable wave.

"I have been trying to do just that all day, but I can't stop thinking about her. Sister…can you help me run away with her?" he pleaded.

"Allah! Not again!" cried Amina, before quickly composing herself. "I myself could have married long ago," she continued. "But I have always turned my suitors away because I wanted to devote myself to you. I will soon be an old spinster. But I don't mind as long as you are right on course for success. Now, you want to lay my efforts and the efforts of our father to waste! And for what? For a marriage that won't work?

"Wake up and stop dreaming! You are a Yibir! Do you know what that means? If you don't know by now, may Allah help you! Don't let the schooling fool you. Ajis will never accept us!"

Amina's argument began so matter-of-factly then turned indignant, as the volume of her voice rose and her nostrils flared and quivered.

"You will be lucky to find a job when you finish school, and I will have pleased the spirit of our father. Listen, you can marry only a girl of your kind. Never fall in love with an Aji woman again. There is a lot that you do not know. In due course, Allah willing, you will know. Just trust me."

Just before she finished, her face relaxed, her mouth opened, her voice broke, and tears streaked down her cheeks.

"Don't cry! Please, don't! I will go to their house tonight and tell her that it can't work," responded Ali. He was not really thinking of what he was saying; it just sounded the right thing to say at the time.

But once he said it, he knew it was a pledge he could not break.

"No!" Amina said. "Don't go to their house. You will not see her again! Write a note and give it to me. I will pass it on to her."

"I will do as you say, sister," he complied meekly.

Then he reached for a notebook, tore out a sheet and began to write in Somali.

Dear Anissa,

Your note tears into my heart. Darling, I love you as much as you do love me. But a marriage between us is not meant to be because I am a Yibir and you are an Aji. The bond that connects me to you cannot withstand the callused hearts and rigid minds that I am fated to face every day, every hour, and every minute of my life. I love you too much to subject you to a life of indignity and rejection. Your love will always be with me. At night, I shall dream of you. I shall groan and grope for you in the dark. In the day, I shall be like a Bedouin roaming the desert under a merciless sun, and you shall be the mirage.

No, I cannot elope with you. Instead, I will pray for you that you will be happy without me. Your happiness is always bliss to me. So wipe your tears away and smile. Smile the smile that has always enchanted me, and just imagine that I am not far away.

Cordially yours,
Ali

He reread the note, shuddering as he came to the last sentence. Suspiring audibly, he handed the note to Amina. Folding it and holding it in one hand, she looked into his eyes. Her other hand reached up and touched his shoulder. For a while, neither spoke. Then she gave a pained smile and left for work.

Saddened but relieved, Amina washed the dishes with as little clatter as possible. Everyone else in the house was now taking a nap.

Amina liked Sahra because she believed that Shara was honest and fair. Sahra never overworked her, as happened to other maids who had the misfortune of working for abusive women. Sometimes, Sahra helped her do the house chores, and Amina never had to work if she were ill—otherwise, Sahra would have been furious had she found out. Still, perhaps even more important for Amina, Sahra never referred to her as a Yibir. In addition, now and then she was kind enough to give Amina a present or a reward, which Amina treasured dearly. Sahra did, on occasion, go into temper tantrums. But these Amina was able to put up with because she knew Sahra was a good person at heart.

Upon finishing the dishes, Amina filled two thermoses with hot tea and milk. Next, she carefully and quietly swept the linoleum floor. Then it was time to do the laundry. By the time she finished washing the clothes, everyone was up and it was time to serve tea.

One of Sahra's two sons, fourteen-year-old Omar, had donned a T-shirt, a pair of shorts, and a pair of sneakers and headed for the school's basketball court. Saleh, Sahra's sixteen-year-old son, waited for his cousin Ibrahim. Sahra was worried about Saleh's association with Ibrahim, her nephew.

As a teenager Ibrahim had grown up in Sahra's house. In his last year of high school, he became obsessed with politics and joined a group of youths infatuated with Marxist doctrine. When he finished high school, he left Sahra's house but was unable to find a job. He still visited occasionally, though, just to have a meal or to have Amina wash his clothes or lately, as was the case that day, to take young Saleh to a newly-formed Marxist circle.

Amina liked Ibrahim as he was before. He had cracked jokes and laughed a lot. Now, however, she could make no sense out of him or what he stood for. She rarely saw him without a book in his hand. Amina remembered one afternoon when he dropped in and sat down on the floor, a few feet away from her. Coolly and methodically, he explained the political realities to her as he saw them.

"You are not getting your labor's worth of pay. You are being exploited. You are shedding blood and sweat; and what are you receiving in return?" he asked angrily.

"I am content," she replied.

"No! You don't understand," he retorted.

With the coolness gone, his eyes were fiery, his face contorted. His neck muscles tensed. And with his voice rising, he went into a long discourse on the surplus value and talked about the *Communist Manifesto* of the nineteenth centurey. He acted or, more correctly, reacted as if this one encounter with a simple, illiterate woman was a defining moment in the proletarian struggle against America and all capitalists worldwide.

"I love my aunt as an aunt. But I have to tell you the truth about her. She is sucking your blood, and like a lamb being led to the slaughter house, you don't even know it," he thundered.

Amina responded by mixing him a cup of orange juice and asking him if he wanted something to eat.

"No!" he snapped petulantly.

He drank the orange juice and then, looking sullen, got up in one abrupt and forceful movement. For a while, he stood erect like a pole before he took two almost superhuman steps and bolted from the house. Amina could only shake her head.

Shara's two daughters, one aged eleven and the other eight, stayed in their room and studied. Now and then, the younger daughter emerged from the room to ask her mother for help with her homework. Then, having received a terse sendoff, she knitted her brows and went back, slapping the book on her knees.

A little after four o'clock in the afternoon, two women arrived: one a close friend of Sahra's named Zeinab, the other a reputed gadabout named Kinsi. Amina served them tea and retired to the kitchen, leaving Sahra and her two visitors in the *dara*, a roofless area in the rear of the house. Amina was shy among outsiders, particularly strangers. Sahra's attempts to draw her into conversations with either group were almost never successful. Amina gave only cursory answers before she retreated into her shell. The longer the visitors stayed the more

Amina immersed herself in deliberately prolonged house chores, all the while keeping her ear cocked for any orders from Sahra. Upon hearing Sahra's call, she would emerge diffidently and stand near the kitchen door, then do whatever was demanded of her. However, when there were no visitors, Amina easily chatted and laughed with members of Sahra's household.

Now, with two visitors in the house, Amina stayed in the kitchen, humming to herself, washing dishes she had already washed, cleaning the kitchen floor, and scrubbing its walls.

Sahra and her guests chatted. *Last week's wedding was a nice one. No, it wasn't nice at all. The food was good, but the dances in the evening weren't. The best female dancers weren't there, and the songs were poor. That was true, but there were lots of people. Was the bride pretty? No, not really. Her cheekbones were too prominent, and she had too much powder on her face. The maid of honor was very pretty though. She shouldn't have been the maid of honor—certainly not for this bride. Did you see the bridegroom? What a man! He had presence all about him. People said he had been in Kuwait for fifteen years. He must have a lot of money. What a lucky girl!*

"By the way, you heard Shukri's daughter Anissa has been given away?" Kinsi asked.

"No," Sahra replied in disbelief. "To whom?"

"To an old man in Saudi Arabia. Shukri received a letter from her husband two days ago," Kinsi explained.

"I wonder how Shukri is taking it. She isn't on good terms with her husband. Every time he comes home on vacation they have a dispute, and elders have to reconcile them. They just don't get along well, and now she has to deal with this!" Zeinab said.

"You don't know Shukri. A few Saudi riyals will turn her head. Even with this man's disreputable history. Do you know what he used to do?" Kinsi asked, now hardly able to contain her enthusiasm.

"I don't even know who the man is. What is his name?" Sahra asked.

"Jibril Warfa Dualeh."

"Never heard of him," Sahra said.

"Well, you couldn't have heard about him because he fled the country twenty-eight years ago. In the year of the *Red Dust*[10] he became a thief. He stole camels, sheep, and goats for their meat. He is a very large man, and he was said to have devoured a camel in three days," Kinsi said.

"He must be a giant of a man...Poor Anissa!" Zeinab commiserated.

Amina was sad for the young girl being thrust onto the lap of an old man she did not even know. She thought about Ali and how diminished he looked when he had finished his note to Anissa. *He will soon get over it*, she thought to herself before the drift of the conversation drew her attention.

"I know something you don't know," Kinsi claimed teasingly.

"Something related to Anissa?" Zeinab asked.

"Yes," Kinsi replied. "There are rumors that she is in love with someone else."

"Who could that be?" asked Zeinab. "Tell us. I thought she was too young to fall in love."

"She's sixteen. Not too young for love," countered Kinsi. "But you can't believe who stole her heart. People say she is under his spell. He must have given her a potion[11]."

Amina knew that Kinsi was talking about her brother and alluding to his being a Yibir. She pricked up her ears and girded up her loins for what most certainly would follow.

"Let's talk about something else," Sahra suggested, somehow sensing Anissa's wooer was none other than Ali. She knew he had tutored her in the past.

Amina resented Sahra's attempt to change the subject. But garrulous Kinsi was not about to be silenced.

Kinsi, her voice lowered but clearly audible through the kitchen door, blurted out the secret. "She is in love with Ali the Yibir."

In a trice, the kitchen door flew open, and before the three women

---

[10] 1950, a year of severe famine and disease in Somalia
[11] Yibirs are thought to be sorcerers.

could even look up, a hard leather sandal struck Kinsi right in the forehead. Blood spurted out. Kinsi jumped to fight. But Zeinab held her back. Sahra struggled with Amina. Her two young girls rushed from their room. The older one joined her mother in trying to restrain Amina.

Realizing she would not be able to get to Amina and take revenge, Kinsi sat down and wailed and beat her chest.

"I, a woman of noble birth, the daughter of Fareh Warsame Addur, hit by, of all people, a Yibir! How dare the woman raise her hand against me? She is not even fit to clean my feet. Woe on to me! Woe on to me!"

Sahra was indignant.

"Don't you ever call her a Yibir again!" she shouted.

"We are Yibirs! But I will never let anybody, no matter who, speak evil of my brother," Amina swore.

Sahra looked at Amina with amused consternation. Turning to Kinsi, now being tended by Zeinab, she explained in a deliberate tone, "No further problems related to this matter! There doesn't seem to be any serious injury. I will compensate you for it. But if you go to the police, I will tell them what you called her. I hope you know the law of the land. They will put you in jail. Right, Zeinab?"

"I am sure it won't come to that. Kinsi will have her forehead checked, and I will let you know what the compensation will be," Zeinab replied.

"I can promise nothing today. I will go home and nurse my wounds," said Kinsi in exaggerated resignation. With gauze and a band on her wound, she rose to her feet and left in a huff with Zeinab.

Back in the kitchen, Amina was so embarassed by what she had just done. *Will Sahra really pay the compensation?* she wondered. But she knew Sahra had always been true to her word.

"What a brave woman! I am glad I have never had a fight with you, Amina. Listen, I will pay her off, but I don't want you to ever trouble her again. The poor woman can't hold her mouth."

"Thanks, for your help. I'm sorry for what I did. I wouldn't have minded if she had said something about me. But it was my brother she was insulting," apologized Amina.

"What a sister!" exclaimed Sahra, as she squatted next to Amina and helped her with the house chores for the rest of the day.

After his note to Anissa, Ali was very much down on himself, depressed and at his wit's end as to what to do. A strong urge to walk conquered him. He walked out and covered quite a distance before finally deciding to sit under a tree. He looked around. The open space and the solitude provided him with a sense of calm. He wished he could commune with anyone or anything that would understand him. Maybe the beasts would understand him, and he would be able to draw solace and comfort from them.

It was getting late in the afternoon, and the silhouette of the tree was long. A lone bird perched on a low branch started to chirp as if to cheer him up. Ali sat cross-legged—his elbows resting on his thighs, his head buried in his hands—and agonized as much for himself as for the angelic Anissa.

"O Allah!" he lamented, "What have I done?"

For almost a year and until barely a day earlier, he had lived the joys of love. Now he was beginning to taste the heartbreak of the loss of love. A Yibir! a Yibir! Damn it! It had all been a fool's paradise!

For the first time in his life he hated himself. Silently, he cursed the moment his father and his mother made love and planted a seed condemned to a life of misery. With Anissa had gone his warm blanket of comfort, leaving him naked and alone. He would always miss the rush of delight he had drawn from her when she had opened the door or when he had heard her voice. Gone were the glowing eyes that had now and then thrown furtive glances meant for him and him alone.

He had, two years earlier, learned the real story of Elmi, the poet who had died of heartbreak over losing the woman he loved to a man who could afford to marry her. Now Elmi's odes to love, which Ali had memorized chapter and verse, had more meaning for him. And the words touched and burned his soul as never before.

He recalled Elmi's full saga of love. Elmi's fateful farewell poem overwhelmed him and unnerved him. He shook his head, willing himself to live and fight Elmi's fatal impulse. And he rose and walked home. It was too soon to die.

The sun was starting to dip. Long streaks of sunlight showed through the branches of the trees and splashed golden on the faded grass. On the horizon, clouds swam in a sea of unreachable, molten gold.

The following day, Ali went to school and learned Anissa had dropped out of school for good. The final nail!

Two thousand miles or so away, an old man with burning loins could hardly contain himself. At night, he stroked his beard and looked up with excited eyes and grinned. Then, aiming up and high with his sword of love, he grunted, "Little gazelle, in a year or two you will be mine!"

Chapter 6

Revelation

It took Ali a few months to recover, somewhat, from a spell of low spirits. Soccer and school helped him pull through, and the dream of college in America was there unabated. Nevertheless, a sense of loneliness haunted him. And he developed an impulsive desire to reach out to both his playmates and classmates.

A new Ali, with two distinct sides to his personality, was emerging. One side of him clung to the dream he had built over the past few years; the other side said, *No! This can't be!*

One side made him happy; the other made him gloomy. As a result, his whole waking hours became hours of struggle to run away from his gloomy side. And his main method of achieving this goal was to be outgoing, genial, and funny.

He became close friends with a boy his age, named Arraleh. Aware of Ali's mood swings, Arraleh went out of his way to try to keep Ali's dark side in check. One day, he decided to invite Ali to a feast celebrating the birth of Arraleh's baby brother. They were both eighteen at the time.

"My parents have asked me to invite my friends," said Arraleh, "and I want you to come. It will be this Friday."

The idea of spending an entire afternoon free from gloomy thoughts appealed to Ali.

"I accept, my friend," Ali said, "I will be there. But I have to tell you that I won't be able to dress for the occasion. I will look like a tramp. I know people dress up for such occasions."

Seeing the validity of Ali's point, Arraleh came up with a suggestion.

"I won't dress up for the occasion either. We both know that dressing up isn't essential. Let whoever thinks you a tramp think me a tramp, too!"

On the night before the feast, Ali did his best to clean his shoes and shine them without shoe polish. He then folded a shirt and a pair of clean but faded trousers neatly and laid them under his pillow. In the morning, he hoped, they would look a lot less wrinkled. Then he slept.

On Friday afternoon, Ali headed towards Arraleh's family's house. It was on the opposite side of the town, where relatively rich people lived. His shirt and his trousers were not wrinkled, but they were worn out. The shirt was missing a button in the middle, exposing his navel. He wore an old sweater over his shirt. The scuffed shoes needed shining. He wore no socks, and he was in need of a haircut. His attempt to comb his curly hair into an Afro was a failure. But he had his muscular physique and his six-foot two-inch height to make him look impressive.

It was a little windy and dry that day. So he avoided areas where, when the wind blew, the dust rose and invaded one's eyes, nostrils, ears, and hair. The streets were deserted, and the shops and teashops were closed for the early afternoon. A boy about his age in greasy khaki trousers and a greasy brown sweater was lazing the afternoon away in the shade of a Nissan truck. A frowzy old man was walking slowly, using a long crooked shaft for support. Now and then, the old man would stop and look around, squinting and using his left hand to protect his eyes from the sun before proceeding slowly without changing course. A blind old lady was leaning against a wall and seemingly whispering to herself, her wizened, wide-open right hand facing up in supplication. A familiar mad man was standing in front of a closed shop, stacks of waste paper in hand, and shouting that the owner of the shop owed him millions.

As Ali came into Arraleh's neighborhood, he was struck by its contrast to his own neighborhood, the shantytown. Here, houses were considerably larger. Following the directions Arraleh had given him, Ali arrived in front of the house in due time and stood before the gate. He knocked. A woman opened it and gasped when she saw him.

"What do you want?" she shouted, blocking the doorway.

"Ar…Arraleh invited me," stammered Ali, already disconcerted by the brusque question and feeling awkward.

Before the woman said anything else, Ali stepped back and quickly looked at the neighboring houses. *Yes, this is the house,* he assured himself before he stepped forward with renewed confidence.

"Arraleh invited you?" she asked, sounding incredulous. "Wait here!"

She went back inside, shutting the gate behind her. Ali was burning with exasperation and on the verge of leaving when the gate opened again and revealed Arraleh smiling, his arms stretched out in a gesture of welcome.

"I am sorry you have been kept waiting," Arraleh apologized. "Let me take you inside."

Arraleh took Ali across a large courtyard. A Land Rover was parked inside. They went across the porch and into a large room. Apparently, most of the guests had already arrived, decked out in their best dresses. Most of them were conversing in groups of two or three or more. Ali had seen many of them at school festivals, soccer matches, or public festivities.

He took his shoes off and stepped into the room, which had been cleared of all chairs and tables. The guests were sitting on beautifully covered mattresses and leaning on pillows lined up against the walls. A wall-to-wall baroque rug and several shiny, smooth calfskins covered the floor. The rug felt nice and soft.

Ali felt like a misfit. Overwhelmed by the lavish splendor around him, he looked for a place to sit among the town's men of pelf and power.

Shortly, the conversations dwindled. Some of the guests murmured. Some looked at Ali furtively. With Arraleh out of the room, he had no one to turn to for comfort. The awkward situation dragged on for about fifteen minutes, making Ali more and more uneasy. Then a man, whom he later came to know was Arraleh's uncle, whispered in his ear, "Let's go to another room."

Breathing a sigh of relief, he followed Arraleh's uncle. The man led him to a smaller, uncarpeted room. Ali sat down on the bare floor. A funny feeling suffused him as he saw and recognized the four men he had just joined. They were all Yibirs. Somewhere in the depths of his soul, a bell rang.

"*Assalamu aleykum*," Ali greeted the four.

"*Wa aleykuma assalam*," they replied, almost in unison.

"Little Ali, I am glad to see you. How are you and Amina doing?" asked one of the four.

"We are both doing well. Thank you. How are you doing, Samatar?"

"Thank Allah, we are doing fine except Halima. She is getting weaker and weaker. Next week, I will go to the countryside and fetch some herbs," Samatar replied, looking pained.

Ali murmured some prayers for the sick woman. But his mind was starting to focus on something else. He studied the faces of the other Yibirs closely and with interest. *I know why I have been brought here.*

His eyes settled on a shaggy old Yibir he had not seen for over two years. The old man had apparently changed little. His hair, uncut and uncombed for years, was in locks. Head heavily furrowed, cheeks crinkled, eyes sunken and rheumy but looking as sharp as an eagle's, the hoary old man presented a hideous specter.

In the past, Ali had felt ashamed of the old Yibir. Aji children contorted their faces, moved their heads in jerks and walked in quick, bouncing steps to ape the old Yibir and by extension mock and taunt Ali. This time, though, Ali felt glad to see him.

"I am glad to see you back, uncle," said Ali, smiling and stretching his hand. The old man smiled back and, shaking Ali's hand, nodded in approval. The old man's hand felt coarse and surprisingly strong.

I know why I have been brought to this room, Ali repeated to himself. He went into a subdued, meditative mood and remained so until he woke up to Arraleh's voice.

"Ali, you are not supposed to be here! My uncle made a mistake. Let's go back in there." Arraleh's voice betrayed a sharp edge.

"No!" Ali replied. "I am quite comfortable here. I am with my uncles and my cousins." As he spoke, Ali felt a weight lift off his shoulders and his chest.

Arraleh could not believe his friend was undisturbed by the obvious indignity. *Hadn't Ali been striving for Aji acceptance?*

To Arraleh's knowledge, Ali had seldom associated with Yibirs and had in fact exhibited noble qualities not seen in Yibirs. He felt that Ali was now risking all he had accomplished.

"Come with me, Ali! Please do! I am begging you," Arraleh pleaded.

"No! We will talk later. Please go and serve your guests," Ali replied emphatically.

Seeing Ali was adamant in his refusal and thinking he must be insane, Arraleh left the room shaking his head.

But Ali knew, right there and then, that a new era was dawning for him. He had always wanted to be not only accepted but also liked by Ajis. And he had thought that the blend of courtesy, shyness, obedience, academic excellence, and athletic prowess would ultimately endear him to them. But, alas, all was for naught! Many of his fellow students respected him; some even liked him. But he now realized that, eventually, they too would turn their backs on him and act like typical Aji adults. Yes, the little respect he was accorded was only ephemeral, and the hard and inescapable reality was that he was a Yibir, plain and simple.

To the sound of laughter, he awoke from his meditative mood. Samatar, Ismail, and Omar were teasing Gureh, the old Yibir, who looked animated. His usual watery eyes were now shining bright, and the facial wrinkles seemed to have vanished under his radiant smile.

"Uncle Gureh, have you thought of marriage lately?" Omar was asking.

"If I do marry, one will not be enough. I will marry four at the same time!" the widowed old man joked. "Never underestimate an old man. A man is a man."

"But could you handle a virgin?"

"The question should be, could a virgin handle me?" Gureh replied, as a fat louse crept slowly down the frayed and greasy collar of his faded shirt.

Attention shifted to Ismail, who had been released from jail only a month earlier. He had been in prison for six months on a murder conviction. The victim, a young boy, had been stabbed to death. A woman swore she had seen Ismail with bloody hands in the vicinity of the crime scene. During court proceedings, Ismail maintained his stony face, a behavior seen unbecoming of a man falsely charged with murder. Fortunately, the victim's family never accepted Ismail as the culprit, and eventually a real witness came forward to implicate the false witness's own husband.

Ali was struck by Ismail's apparent lack of bitterness and the ease and humor with which the Yibirs treated his unjust imprisonment. The atmosphere grew convivial to such a point that everything that was said led to laughter. Ali was astonished that the Yibirs were engaging, sensitive, and very human, unlike any he had known. Gone were their Sphinx faces and reticent tongues. And they were witty, intelligent men and seasoned graduates of the school of hard knocks—men who bore considerable weight on their broad shoulders well. But just as Ali was pondering this new illuminating knowledge, Arraleh's uncle came in. Then, suddenly, the merry faces gave way to stern and stony faces.

It was as if each Yibir had two personalities: one for the Aji world, the other for the Yibir world. Among Ajis, the Yibir was a masked dissembler who stolidly hid his pain as well as his pleasure. Among his own people, however, the Yibir came out and showed his true self, his heart and his humanity. The Ajis could therefore never know the Yibir, which served the Yibir just well.

Ali felt strangely relaxed, at ease with himself. School, soccer, and false hopes had long shielded him from his people. Now that he was talking freely to his fellow Yibirs, it felt like he had just found long lost relatives. And he wondered why he had never taken time to know his people.

Two people came in: one holding a trencher brimming with rice and chunks of boiled mutton, the other carrying a bowl of water. The trencher and the bowl of water were set side by side on the floor. There was one large knife in the trencher. The characteristic aroma of ghee prepared with mint filled the air. One at a time, all five Yibirs dipped hands into the bowl of water, in descending order of age.

Samatar took the knife and cut the large chunks of meat into smaller pieces. Then they said, "In the name of Allah," and started to eat. Using their right hands to pick up the food, they ate slowly and quietly and made sure they left some food in the dish.

When they finished eating they said, "Praise be due to Allah," and washed their hands in the same order as before.

After the food, the Yibirs waited for the host. Wishing he could leave, Ali grew restless. He knew what was about to happen, and he resented it. He made a move for the door. Old Gureh stopped him. Should he stay and accept the stamp of ignominy? Or should he flout the old man's order and reject his people? He chose to stay.

Presently, Arraleh's father, Arraleh's uncle, and Arrlaeh himself appeared. Two women followed them in. The tall woman must be Arraleh's mother, thought Ali; and indeed she was.

Arraleh's father said, "I understand that you have been fed," rather imperiously.

"Yes, we have been fed," Gureh replied, impassively.

Arraleh's father produced a wad of bills of money and said, "It is for the five of you."

"We accept it," Gureh said, without counting the money.

Witnessing the traditional reception of the propitiatory *customary gift*[1], Ali was both nervous and curious.

Gureh started a benediction for the newborn and his family. "Amen," said Arraleh.

"*Don't* say 'Amen!'" admonished the two women.

Without batting an eye, Gureh continued the benediction. Ali was shocked. It had never occurred to him that anyone could so discourteously reject a prayer.

He studied the faces of the people around him. Gureh continued to pray without any show of emotion. Arraleh's father looked impatient and checked his watch repeatedly. Arraleh's uncle wore an unsettling look of disgust and contempt. The two women looked on anxiously and studied the faces of the Yibirs and listened keenly for anything that might suggest an evil rune. Arraleh's eyes welled with tears. The three remaining Yibirs looked glum.

[1] Bu Ur Ba Avr's bloodmoney (See the prologue)

The scene was rich in contrast and irony. Simplicity in form clashed with complexity in substance. The past dominated the present. Close physical proximity emphasized deep social division. Dissonant moods dishonored the birth of a child. The tormented and their tormentors stood face to face, united by a common compulsive desire to end the occasion and part quickly.

After Gureh had finished the prayers, the five Yibirs were herded out of the room, through a back door, and out of the house.

What an uncivil sendoff! thought Ali.

As he stepped out, he looked back, almost involuntarily. Arraleh was following them, lethargically and gloomily, to see them out. Ali's and Arraleh's eyes met. Then, as if on cue, Arraleh's tears broke out and coursed down his cheeks. Looking away, he cried silently. There was no good bye, and as far as anybody could tell the two never spoke again.

A few minutes later the five Yibirs separated. Ali headed home. The twenty shillings in his pocket gave him a strange feeling. The whole episode and his acceptance of the customary gift, which he gave to Amina, nauseated him. But he felt no shame. And he bore no sense of gratitude to Arraleh's father.

The day's bitter revelation kept him on edge. He had never realized that rejection of Yibirs ran so deep. When night came, he could not concentrate on his homework. At bedtime, he had difficulty sleeping. And the closed window of the house denied him a soporific gaze at the stars.

They think we are so evil that our only purpose in life is to put curses on people. To them, we are too spiritually unclean for God to answer our prayers—we can communicate only with evil spirits. It is not enough that through the centuries we have been turned into beings little better than slaves. They see us as a menace, and they would rather have us disappear. The customary gift is a tool to keep us down, down, down, and at bay.

The more he thought about it the angrier and the more frustrated he grew, until he fell asleep from sheer exhaustion.

Amina woke him up.

"You are almost late for school," she said in a scolding tone.

He jumped to his feet, got ready, ate breakfast quickly, and dashed out the door. Then, checking how high the sun was, he slowed down to a brisk walk. But as soon as he caught his breath and calmed down, the dreadful feelings of the night before rushed back like a bitterly cold draft.

At the accursed spot where his father had taken final leave of him, he slowed his pace. Feeling sad and somber, slowing down and look-ing south had long been his ritual to mark their parting. The usual forlorn feeling now had an unusual edge to it. He was overcome with self-pity.

I was born a Yibir. I was nine when my father died. My mother I can't even remember. Nobody wants me except my sister and poor Anissa, whom I have lost forever. Anissa, Anissa, I still have a tender place for you in my heart…Nobody has ever told me how my mother died. My sister doesn't want me to know. Yibir, Yibir, Yibir! Why so much humil-iation and misery. God, why, why?

O God, I have sinned! I have questioned your infinite wisdom. O God, forgive me! I love you; I fear you, and I believe in you. But why is this happening to us? What have we done to have incurred Your wrath?

Despondent and deeply agitated, he arrived at school unable to shake off the nagging question, Why is this happening to us? Associated with this question came the fear of heresy. Had he not been taught that all was preordained? Why was he questioning God's wisdom and divine justice?

The questions would not go away. And the more he wished them to go away the more inexorable they became. They kept bobbing up and stubbornly sticking to his mind. They were on his mind when he sat down and a teacher started a lecture. They were there during the breaks. They were there after school. They were there on his way home. They were there at home and at night. They were there the following day, and they were there to stay, and the longer they stayed the more virulent they became.

In the days and weeks that followed, Ali's inner turmoil began to affect his mood. The dark side he had been running away from finally caught up with him. He became a distrait boy with a quick temper. In all his waking hours, except the first few minutes after a good night's sleep, he combated anger, sadness and despair. A lump gnawed at his throat and made it feel constantly sore. And he felt tired all the time. He hated his waking hours. He hated his nights, when he closed his eyes and tried to sleep. He hated to be alone. He hated to be with people, feeling they might perceive all that went on inside him. He was no longer able to focus on anything for any significant stretch of time. His mind had to battle with questions that attacked him relentlessly. The questions that fought their way into his mind varied in complexity and relevance, but they were all equally vexing. No sooner one nagging question left his mind than another took its place, or an older one returned with a vengeance.

Within a month, he was in a twilight zone. The constant tug of war took possession of his mind, and he was unable to answer any question with certitude.

Have I locked the door? Not sure! Check and check and check. I am still not sure. Never mind. Just check fifteen times and remember the number… Have I washed my hands? Just wash them five times and remember the number…Did I turn in the homework this morning? Yes, I did. How do I know? I pinched my thigh as I handed it to the teacher. I remember the pain of the pinching. So the pinching worked! But, still, I don't have that sense of certitude I used to have and other people surely have…

Do I love my sister? Yes, I do. I know I do. But now that the question has come up, I have lost the feeling of love for her. This horrifies me because it is my sister I am talking about. Try it. Try it. Try it. No, no, no, I can't… I will regain that warm and comforting and joyous feeling for my sister when the question leaves my mind. But when will that be? When an equally troublesome question comes along and rams into my head…

Have I solved this exam problem correctly? Have I put down 25 as the answer? Look at the answer. It is 25. Look at it again and again. Look at it ten more times and remember the number 10. Now, move on to the next exam problem. But have I written my name on the sheet?

I feel angry with myself all the time...

I am losing my mind! I am losing my mind! I can see myself going insane, and shedding my clothes. I can see myself running naked in the streets. I can see people shouting, Catch him! Catch him! I can feel the people catching me and carrying me, all of me, my four limps flailing in the air. They are carrying me to the mad house. I can hear the steel door slamming behind me...That wouldn't be as dreadful as it sounds. I would be able to bang my head against the silent walls and shout my frustrations out. The things that bother me now wouldn't bother me then. They bother me now because I care. But if I were mad and seen as mad, I wouldn't care what I thought and what other people thought of me. I would be expected to follow no rules. And all that doesn't make sense now would make perfect sense in the unfettered, serene world of madness.

But my sister would hurt and cry and be heartbroken. I don't ever want my sister in the condition I found her in when my father died and I came back from school. Besides, if people actually take me to the mad house, they will label me "mad" and never give me a chance at sanity again. No! No! I will not let them do that to me. I will not let them destroy my sister. I just want to be normal again and to live a normal life.

One evening, Ali walked out after supper without telling Amina where he was going. About an hour later, he stormed into the house raging like a bull.

"Tell me! Tell me!" he shouted.

"No!" Amina cried. "You are not ready!" She knew what he was talking about.

It was their first reference to what to him was a suffocating mystery and to her a painful secret.

"I need to know. I want to know," he said, plaintively.

"Patience! Patience! You are not ready for the truth!"

"You have been dealing with it for so long. Why can't I?"

"I can deal with it because I have *lived* it. You see, with me, there has never been a choice. It was forced on me."

"But you have left me in the dark. I want to break out of it. I want to be free. Tell me the truth! Tell me the truth!"

"It is only a matter of time."

A faraway, sullen look was constantly showing on his face. His eyes looked deep and unresponsive because he could only look inwards, not outwards. He looked into a world of dells and narrow and dark alleys and peaks and valleys and caves, a world that felt and looked horrifyingly real in his mind, a world with no place to sit or rest, an unshakeable world of constant fear and ultimate solitude. People saw his expression of pain, suggestive of stomach ailment, and his immense distress broken only by rare moments of intense excitement.

He soliloquized. He did not mind soliloquizing when alone. But it embarrassed him deeply when people noticed he was talking to himself. It was amazing how even when he barely twitched a small part of a lip, to commune with himself, people noticed and looked at him queerly. Long, brisk walks in the wilderness seemed to help, but only temporarily, for brisk walks in the real world never translated into brisk walks in the gloomy world of his cavernous mind. And the violent shakes of his head—attempts to shake out the demons that had taken residence there—never worked.

This time around, no one knew how to extricate Ali from his misery. The principal, whom Ali now considered something of a friend, did not know how to help him. The teachers saw his deteriorating condition and watched in sadness. And Amina was a distressed witness to his fall into a deep dark hole of gloom.

Chapter 7

The Last Straw

Soccer became Ali's only passion. The spinning sphere with the magical feel was something he could focus on and enjoy. He had developed immense skills that made him a soccer star in the province at a time soccer was gaining popularity in the whole country.

His coach wanted him to play left wing, as no other player on his team was able to handle this position. Tall and strong, he had an elegant way of running. Starting slowly and stealthily as he deftly positioned himself, he would often explode with a burst of energy and speed as he received the ball from a teammate or snatched it from an opponent. His passes were neat and accurate, his dribbling a beauty to behold, his shot into the opposing goal hard and deadly. He turned into a well-oiled soccer machine most renowned for his heroics in tight games. And in soccer he became a source of pride for the town. Yet, deep within his mind, torment reigned and ran amok.

In the middle of the summer before Ali's last year of high school, there was a soccer match between the team from his province and that of a neighboring one. Ali was the only high school student on the team. At eighteen years of age, he looked stronger than most of the other players, who were in their twenties and early thirties.

The game was scheduled to start at 4:00 p.m. At 2:30 that afternoon, Ali woke up from a short nap and washed, in preparation for the game. After prayers, he had a cup of hot tea without milk or sugar. The prospect of the game had already created a great deal of excitement in him. He was tense. But the pregame tension was a welcome relief from his usual despondency. He took his time sipping the tea. When he finished, he got into the soccer gear the team had loaned him for the game. A red jersey with white stripes, a white pair of shorts, thick white socks edged with red stripes, and a pair of white and black

Adidas soccer shoes heightened his anticipation for the game.

He locked the door, then checked and rechecked it a number of times to make sure it was locked before heading toward the shanty-town. To his right, vultures were feasting on a carcass. He stopped to take a good look. A crow flew by. Undaunted, the vultures continued to dig into the carcass with their sharp beaks. Ali soon approached the shacks. Women and children standing by the doors and tiny windows of their hovels followed his progress. He was aware of their watchful eyes on him, and he walked with a sense of pride he had rarely felt before. The Adidas beat rhythmically on the hard surface and imbued him with a sense of buoyancy and invincibility. A young woman began to ululate. An elderly lady silenced her with a curt "shut up!"

The playground on the town's side of the shacks was deserted, a testament to the game's importance. The match was going to be held in the newly built soccer stadium, which stood on a grassy clearing between the town and the government quarters.

Few teashops were open, and almost no customers could be seen in them. At one street corner, two elderly men in turbans squatted on the ground and played *shah*[2]. At the approaching sound of heavy footsteps, one of the men looked up, only to see a grown man in shorts. He squinted in puzzlement and shook his head in disgust, then looked down to make his next move.

Near the center of the town, Ali was joined by two of his team-mates—one, like Ali, wearing a red jersey with white stripes, the other wearing the traditional black jersey of the goalie. They could see people moving en masse toward the stadium. A mad woman with a game foot hobbled forth, using a long shaft for support, and moved fast. She sang an old war song that in the olden days women sang to cheer their men on in battle. Ali and his friends looked at each other and laughed heartily.

Suddenly, the mad woman stopped and stood erect like a squirrel.

"You laughing at me?" she asked. "Laugh at your own mothers!" Then, she continued to limp and sing, not caring to know who the men in shorts were.

---

[2] Somali chess

Closer to the stadium, the ululation and the singing and the drum beating gave a fitting prelude to the game. The lines were still long, and there were many policemen manning the gates, keeping their eyes on the swelling crowd. Packs of children chirruped like excited birds and hovered around the gates. A number of government Land Rovers, guarded by another group of alert policemen, were parked outside the stadium. All in all, the atmosphere and the prevailing mood were those of a joyous fiesta.

The opposing players entered through the side doors and went into their respective rooms. Ali and his two companions were the last to arrive. Having gone over the plan with all the players the day before, the coach used ten minutes for a pep talk. He reminded his boys of the stinging defeat the province's team had suffered the year before at the hands of today's opposing team. (Ali had been deemed too young to be on that defeated team of the year before. But the defeat was a defeat for the entire province, no matter who had been on the team the year before.)

The moment of truth was near. Some of the players prayed silently. Some kept to themselves and assumed solemn faces. Others affected merriment, laughed, and poked fun at one another. Ten minutes before game time they all took to the field. The air was still, and it was a warm and sunny day. The bright sunlight shone on the brilliantly colored dresses of the women. The singing and the shouting and the drum beating rose sharply and excited the players and the crowd even more. The governor and the mayor and other high-ranking government officials were present. Men and women, young and old were there. And it seemed that all the children had managed, after all, to get into the stadium, filling the stands with bird-like warbles and sparkling eyes on cherubic faces.

On the field, the players trotted, sprinted, and stretched and hopped up and down. The opposing teams intermingled. Some shook hands and talked. When it was time to start the game, the twenty-two players took their positions on the field. A shrill whistle signaled the start of the much-anticipated match.

The supremacy of the visiting team was soon evident. Its players seemed better conditioned, and they had a playmaker, Saeed, who was strong, energetic, and creative. The midfielders of the town's team were no match for Saeed and unable to feed the forwards and the wings. Playing left wing, Ali saw little of the ball. And he could not roam the field or be creative with the ball as he would have liked. Fifteen minutes into the game, Saeed received the ball in the middle of the field. Dribbling around two opponents, he passed the ball to a teammate running alongside him. Saeed then slipped through the line of defenders, just in time to receive the ball with his left foot and shoot with his right—a classic goal.

The coach had to make a quick decision because it was clear that Saeed's creativity was taking his team apart. He decided to play the only card he had and switched Ali to midfield. Ali was not as strong or seasoned as Saeed, but he was faster. The town's team soon settled down and began to play with more poise and precision. And the game began to turn into a duel between Ali and Saeed. The crowd sensed an unfolding drama. There was the time when Ali stole the ball and maneuvered between two players only to find Saeed in his path. The trick that Ali played on the more seasoned player left the latter ridiculously contorted and brought a roar of approval from the crowd.

But then Ali, having not given up the ball quickly enough, lost it. At that moment, Ali's captain, who had been expecting a pass, got into Ali's face.

"Stupid and selfish Yibir!" the captain said. Only Ali could hear what the captain said.

Cut to the quick, Ali froze in his tracks and stared at his captain in disbelief. For a moment, he stood still. The comment had jarred him to the bone. The sanctity of the sport had just been violated. His last refuge had been invaded. On the grandest stage of his life, he was being dumped like trash. He could never have imagined such naked insensitivity, let alone been prepared for it. Alas, the sport he had loved and that had given him so much, was not the sanctuary he had thought it was. He looked around and saw not fellow soccer players and a cheering crowd but poisonous vipers.

They had already destroyed his dreams. And now they would not let him keep his one remaining passion. Only one thing remained for him to do. He walked off the field.

Unaware of what had just transpired on the field and utterly non-plussed, the coach ran after Ali. Reserves and fans followed him. The coach caught up with Ali just before the gate.

"You can't leave the game like that! What is the matter with you?" the coach screamed.

"Just stay out of my way!" Ali replied, coldly and emphatically.

"No! No! I can't let you go. Tell me what happened out there!" the coach shouted.

What the coach had no way of knowing was that this was not the same Ali he had known. Over the last minute or two, Ali had accomplished what he had never had enough will or courage to accomplish. He had jumped off the fence that stood between Ajis and Yibirs and landed plainly and squarely on the Yibir side. And he wanted the world to see.

Ali looked at his coach and saw not the humble, honest man he had known but a crocodile.

What could this man understand? Ali asked himself. He then snarled and shoved the coach so hard that the coach fell flat on his back and looked up with startled eyes. Two policemen, who had been holding the surging crowd back, charged at Ali and shouted, "Stop! You are under arrest!"

Ali faced the two policemen and snorted. With a sneer on his face, he proceeded to walk as if nothing had happened. Just then, the principal arrived and convinced the two policemen to let Ali go. The mad woman with the game foot appeared and flailed with her shaft at the crowd.

"Shame on you!" she scolded the crowd. "Don't you see the man is on his way to the bathroom? Leave him alone! Let the man relieve himself!"

The crowd in the immediate vicinity, including the policemen, laughed. Ali paused momentarily to throw one curious and amused look at the crippled mad woman, who was now singing away and dancing in honor of the town's team.

The principal talked to the coach and accompanied him to the bench. The crowd in the stadium stood as if shocked and dismayed.

And their team was dealt a humiliating defeat.

From the stadium, Ali headed straight home. As he walked, scenes from his life flashed by. He saw his father walking south and disappearing behind the hills on that fateful journey. He saw Amina lying curled up, in shock on that dreadful day. He thought of the time he was frozen out by his classmates. He thought of the time the neighborhood kids assailed him and drove him away. Images of his altercation with the bigger boy—when Amina had to resort to the then stupefying but now understandable tactic to save his life—flickered before his eyes. He thought of the way he and the other Yibirs were treated in Arraleh's house. And he thought of many other incidents in which it had been made clear to him that he did not belong.

I have always asked myself why people are so cruel to us. I should, instead, ask why we want to be part of them.

A strange and ominous calm descended upon him. To be sure, he was still angry, as he had been so many times before in the face of naked prejudice. This time, however, it was not the kind of anger that was born of frustration, and that led to more frustration. Rather it was the kind of anger that tended to concentrate one's emotional energy on one supremely important point. It was the kind of anger associated not with mental obfuscation. It was the kind of anger that gave rise to extraordinary mental clarity and steely resolve.

He resolved that he would withdraw from a society that loathed him and his people. There was no reason, he thought, to remain in school. At the time, the schools were closed, and he had but one year to go in secondary school. But he saw that, in the eyes of society, a Yibir who happened to be a high school graduate was still a Yibir and would continue to be treated as such.

I am glad I know enough to read and write sufficiently well, which is all I need. A secondary school diploma has no substance to a Yibir. In future, I shall read all the books I can lay my hands on and talk to my people and get them organized. I shall teach every Yibir child to hold his head high and be proud of his Yibirness. No more false dreams! It is time to face reality.

Chapter 8

Secret Unveiled

Truth harms not. It only shocks.
— Somali proverb

By the time Ali reached home, he was a changed man. He waited for his sister to arrive. When she arrived, she served him supper. Then he walked out.

Amina had been well briefed about the incident at the stadium by Sahra's sons. But she chose not to make an issue of it. For quite some time now, she had known that her brother was under the sway of currents beyond his or her control. She had hoped that there would soon be an auspicious time when she would have to talk and he would have to listen. Ali's drastic action at the stadium and his subsequent calm and resolute demeanor were an indication that now was the time.

For two hours, Ali traipsed the wilderness in the dark. He felt curiously relieved and at one with the nocturnal beasts. A little before nine o'clock, he returned and found Amina sitting on her mat. She looked serious. He knew that she wanted to talk, and he braced himself for a sharp reprimand.

"Sit down!" Amina commanded. "I will fetch you a cup of tea."

He sat on his mat. She went into the kitchen and came back with a cup of tea. He began to take a sip.

"Ali, listen carefully," Amina started. "I am about to tell you something I have never told you before."

Raising his eyebrows a little, Ali eyed Amina with curiosity. *She probably received a proposal of marriage and wants to share it with me*, he thought. A knowing grin showed on his face and eased his tension.

"It is about time you were told the story of our family," explained Amina. She then coughed slightly.

Ali nearly jumped out of his skin and almost dropped the tea cup. *Could the gaping hole collapse? Could the dead come back and talk?* His eyes bulging, lower jaw dropping, mouth gaping, he looked at Amina in disbelief.

The story of his family had until now been off-limits to him. His family was one with a dark side, a story he had always viewed with both dread and desire. Now was the moment when the past would be illuminated. Now was the moment when his existence would begin to make sense to him. Now was the moment to enliven a part of him that had grown stunted, distorted, diseased, unreachable, and very, very dark. Yet, when that moment of a lifetime was finally upon him, he was totally unprepared.

What is she going to say? He girded up his loins and with a bated breath waited for her to begin.

Amina coughed again and held her chest gently. She waited for the irritation to subside. Then, in a sober and even tone, she began to tell the story of the family.

"A long time ago, in the Year of the Red Dust, our father left Las Burgabo. He had lost his parents, his three siblings and many of his other close relatives to famine and disease. He settled in a town very far away, where nobody knew him…

"He was a skilled mason. But now he was ready to start at the bottom as a handyman for masons…People soon found out he was good at his work. Someone asked him to build a house. He built the best house in town.

"He talked little and never told people he was a Yibir. People liked him and just assumed he was an Aji.

"At some point, a wealthy man named Hajji Dualeh asked Father to build a house for him. The house took about one year to build. But that year was the most fateful of our father's life.

"Dualeh's eldest daughter saw him and liked him. She often visited the site where Father was building the house. Father liked her, too. The two grew close until one spring afternoon she told Father that she liked him and wanted him to marry her. Father was shocked.

She was an Aji; he was a Yibir! *How could they marry?*

"He felt sorry for the young woman, so he told her the truth. 'I am a Yibir,' he said. Halima still wanted him to marry her. Father told me that he then asked her to run away with him. She refused and insisted that they be wed in her hometown. She also asked Father to present himself as an Aji...Father agreed.

"Father lied to Hajji Dualeh and his family and married Halima. For twelve years they lived a good life together. They had four children: first me, then Sahra, then Mahad, and last you. Sahra was two years younger than me. Mahad was three years younger than Sahra. You came four years after Mahad. *We are Halima's children!*"

For the first time in his life, Ali knew the name of his mother. Until now, everything about her had been a mystery to him. The unfolding drama gripped the totality of his being: mind, body and spirit. And it felt as if every pore and every cell of his body had opened up to receive his roots. It was the past talking to him. It was his mother reaching from the grave, at last, to touch him and reveal herself. It was a tangle of life and death dancing together and taunting and teasing and testing him.

"We lived in a stone house that Father had built," Amina continued. "Mother liked the country better. I remember several springs she took us to the countryside to live with the nomads. Father always stayed behind in town, in those times...

"How I loved those times! I liked the fresh milk and fresh honey and clean air. I ran around in the open grasslands, among the goats and the sheep and the birds and the grasshoppers and the blooming shrubs and trees. But that was before you were born...

"I remember our grandfather, Hajji Dualeh. He was a turbaned man, and he fingered his prayer beads a lot. His way of greeting me was to smile and kiss me on the cheek and gently pat my head with his right hand. But he rarely talked, and we rarely saw him or our uncles.

"Grandmother, though, was a big part of our life. She and Aunt Maryam, Mother's younger sister, entertained us children and helped our mother. There was a time when you wouldn't take food from any hand except Grandmother's. I remember Grandmother as short and strong…She liked to hold her family together…close together.

"Aunt Maryam was a cheerful woman. She was tall like her father and she was pretty and she liked to sing when she did the house chores. She took me around and showed me places and taught me all the stories I know. Aunt Maryam was often with us, and we liked to be with her. It was a happy life of proud and loving adults and cheerful children laughing and running around, enjoying love and simply being together.

"Then one day, about sixteen years ago, it all came apart. Someone who had known Father came to town and found out what had happened. He went straight to our uncles and told them the truth about Father…The brothers met to discuss the matter in secret. They decided that one of them should go to Las Burgabo with a picture of Father. He came back with the news that Father was indeed a Yibir…

"The world of our family turned up side down and our fate was sealed. They declared our family a shame they had to destroy. Our flesh and blood disowned us and decided to wipe us out in the middle of the night."

Somewhere in Ali's mind, the tangle of life and death danced ominously and sang the song of death.

"At the time of the satanic decision, Grandmother, Father, you, and I were at home. Mother and the other two children were visiting a family in another part of the town. The decision was taken in the house of one of our uncles…

"Aunt Maryam was there. She heard all that was said. But she acted as though she didn't know what was happening and then slipped out of the house. She ran the whole distance to our house…

"After all these years, I still remember! She was out of breath when she arrived. I remember her face…She talked to Grandmother…Father heard Aunt Maryam's screams and incoherent talk. He came out of the room to find out what was happening. Grandmother turned to him.

" 'Are you a Yibir?' she asked him. 'Yes,' he replied without hesitation. For a short while, Grandmother didn't talk. Then, she said, 'It was God's will that my daughter was married to you. And your children are a testament to the will of God. You are like a son to me.'

"I still remember every single word that she said.

"Grandmother commanded us to flee for our lives. 'Don't wait for my daughter and the other two children. If it is God's will that they die, they will die! Maryam, stuff what you can in that little bag and fill one plastic bottle with water and another with milk. I will stand outside and watch.'

"Yes. That's what she said…

"Father made the second most fateful decision of his life. He…He decided to save you and me!"

For the first time since she had began the story, Amina's voice cracked. A lump rose to her throat. She paused and took a deep breath before continuing.

"Frantic moments followed. Aunt Maryam and Father ran back and forth. They said little. I cried…You cried. Aunt Maryam tried to calm you down and calm me down. A little after dusk, the small bag was full. A plastic bottle of milk and another of water lay beside the bag…Father got his rifle. You were secured to his back with a white sheet of cloth…He slung the gun over his right shoulder and held the bag and the bottle of milk in his left hand. The bottle of water was wrapped in a cloth and strapped onto my shoulders.

"Up to that point Grandmother hadn't shed a tear. Aunt Maryam had long stopped crying. Then when it was time to leave, the quiet wailing began. Tears flowed. Grandmother prayed, and we all kissed one another…Then Father, you, and me slipped out into the dark night to wherever God might take us…

"We left Mother and Sahra and Mahad behind."

Suddenly the tangle of life and death stopped dancing, and there was only death. Short of breath, Ali worked his heaving lungs to gasp for air.

"So it was murder? Bloody murder?" he cried

"Yes! It was bloody murder!" she replied.

He had thought he had found her. The brother and the sister, too! But it had been only a brief encounter. Their receding faces slipped away beyond the reach of his restless soul. And it was the return of darkness—only one of a different sort. Now a shrine of trapped souls and suspended lives and frozen time and betrayed hearts and decaying bones, the thick mass of darkness stood as a pulsating force of a damning evidence and a painful truth.

To Ali, the story's sudden twist towards disaster felt like having the ground cut from under his feet. His trancelike state broke. A frantic look came over his face. He reached towards Amina and touched her forehead and felt her face and held her hand. Her hand trembled. His hand trembled, too. Their eyes met, and they exchanged sad but knowing looks.

"We walked in the direction of the bush first," Amina went on. "Once in the bush, we turned north. At first, I didn't feel anything but fear and sadness. I...I was old enough to know what was going to happen to Mother and the little ones..." She paused.

"We pulled away from the town. I felt cold. I needed a blanket, but there was no blanket... You slept most of the way that first night...It was hard to keep pace with Father. He had to slow down every once in a while so that I could catch up. Just before dawn, I was too tired to walk, and Father decided to rest.

"I wanted to sleep on my mattress, and I wanted to feel my mother's warmth before I slept. But we were far away, too far away, from the comfort I had known. We had walked at least twenty miles, and we were near the far edge of the bush. I think another reason we stopped was that we were heading into open land. Father didn't want us to cross in the daylight.

"We sat down. My shoulders ached. Father fed you. I didn't take a single sip of water or milk...I lay on the cool, dewy ground and immediately went into a deep sleep.

"When I woke up, I was shocked to find myself lying in the wilderness. But I came to my senses fast. I remembered the events of the night before. I...I knew that you and I were now motherless children.

"Father was sitting and holding you in his lap. You were reaching with your tiny fingers for his mouth, daring him to bite them and, then, withdrawing them at the last moment as he playfully lunged with his open mouth. At that moment of grief and fear, you made both Father and me laugh. Father later told me that at that very moment he just felt and believed that we were somehow going to survive…

"As soon as Father saw that I was awake, he gave me two mouthfuls of water and two mouthfuls of milk. And he massaged my stiff and aching feet. I knew that he was conserving most of the water and the milk for you. Father and I would have to do with as little as possible. I later realized that Father hadn't taken a sip of water or milk, and that he had been up all night.

"Late in the morning, we moved to the shade of a large tree. Father told me to be on the lookout while he slept. His right hand still held the gun…

"This was the first time you asked me about the rest of the family. You kept saying, 'Where is Mother? Where is Sahra? Where is Mahad? Where is Grandmother? Where is Aunt Maryam?' I kept telling you that we were on our way to the countryside and that the rest would catch up with us. You cried…Father woke up. I held you and rocked you and sang to you. When you slept, I laid you beside Father.

"Only then could I begin to think clearly. I was terrified. I could see the faces of Mother, Mahad, and Sahra…I had no way of knowing where we were heading or what would become of us. And it was hard to think of life without Mother and Sahra and Mahad…without Grandmother and Aunt Maryam.

"Before noon, Father woke up and found me asleep leaning against the tree trunk. We hid in the bush the whole day and resumed walking at sunset. I soon realized it was going to be a lot harder than the night before. I tired a lot faster, and it was colder than the night before…I shivered. You slept most of the time, covered with a blanket.

"I thought of what might have happened to our mother and our brother and our sister…I cried the whole night, mostly silently but sometimes loudly. Every now and then, Father had to pause and hug me and calm me. He tried to keep a happy face whenever he looked at me…*He was a Yibir*. He knew how to be strong.

"We weren't able to cover as much distance as the previous night because of my condition. We stopped a little after midnight. Father kindled a fire. The fire kept us warm, and we kept feeding the fire with dry twigs. Father spent the night on the lookout. I later learned that the area was known to be filled with lions and hyenas. Thank God, we didn't encounter any.

"I had nightmares all night. I dreamed of angry men shaking guns and spears and daggers…I heard Mother's screams. She begged her brothers for mercy before her head was cut off and Sahra and Mahad were stabbed with spears…Other times, I saw blood…lots of blood flowing like a river. And I saw a huge fire.

" Other times, I heard men laughing and felt them advancing and receding in the dark… I still remember Father shaking me out of my nightmares and reassuring me that all was going to be well…But when I went back to sleep, the nightmares returned.

"At sunrise, we packed our belongings and started walking again. I was hungry and thirsty and so tired. I could barely walk. Every muscle in my body ached. My legs felt heavy. I could not tell whether I was carrying my legs or my legs were carrying me. I don't know what was driving me… I walked and walked and walked until I was unable to walk, and I collapsed.

"We had little water and little milk left. Father gave me a mouthful of water and a mouthful of very sour milk. Then he laid you and me in the cool shade of a large tree. He took the large sheet of cloth he had been carrying and climbed the tree until he reached one of the higher boughs. He built a hammock and then came down… When he reached the ground, he just looked at me without saying a word…

"He lifted his head, face upward, and prayed. For the first time in my life, I saw tears running down his cheeks. I cried too. He turned towards me and spoke to me…he was shaking.

" 'My daughter,' he said, 'I will take you up the tree and put you in that hammock! I will walk as fast as I can to a town, about one-day's journey away. I will leave you the little milk we have left, but I will keep the water for the baby. If Allah is willing that we survive, I will get back to you in two days. You must never get out of the hammock until you hear a human voice, hopefully my voice. Our dear God, the Lord of Adam and Noah and Abraham and Moses and Joseph and

Jesus and Muhammad, the Compassionate and Munificent Lord of the universe shall not forsake us, and it is in His care that I leave you. My daughter, pray, pray, pray, and all shall be well!'"

Amina paused and took a deep breath. A profound meditative look came over her face. Outside, it was very, very dark and very quiet. All Ali could hear was the throbbing of his overwhelmed heart.

"Father took me up the tree and laid me in the hammock…He laid the bottle of milk beside me and then climbed down and secured you to his back and moved away…He…He never looked back—not even once!

"He walked away in long strides…To this day, I can still see Father's broad shoulders and you secured to his back, looking like a tiny leather bottle…You turned your neck and looked up and gazed at me."

A smile showed on Amina's face.

"I kept looking at you until you were too far away for me to tell that it was you I was watching. You and Father disappeared. I was alone… I was terrified.

"Father walked without rest. He was surprised at how much energy he had left…He kept thinking about me, and the more he thought about me, the faster he walked away from me!

"Afterwards, he said he always felt God had driven him on. How else could he have covered a twelve-hour journey in only about six hours?

"He reached the nearest town at about midnight. But before he entered the town, he hid the gun in the bush. Then, after asking for directions, he headed for the police station. The policemen at the station were appalled by your and Father's conditions. They immediately sent a foot messenger to a small clinic. A nurse came in a Land Rover. She tried to take you and Father to the clinic. Father refused attention but turned you over to them and begged the policemen to send help to me.

"The sergeant ordered three policemen to go with Father in a Land Rover and rescue me. They were to drive the Land Rover as far as they could. Two policemen and Father would then go on foot and look for me.

"Remember I told you that I kept looking at you until you disappeared? I still kept looking in the same direction until it was dark and cold. I became even more terrified. But then I had recollections of happier times with Mother and Sahra and Mahad and you and Father and Grandmother and Aunt Maryam and Grandfather and even our uncles.

"I was in this unreal world and about to doze off when a thunderous roar came from under the tree. I nearly fell off my hammock. I held on tightly. The roar continued for almost half the night. I felt it was going to be the end of me. I thought of Father coming back only to find bits and pieces of his one remaining daughter... I held on. The roaring ceased at about midnight, and I fell asleep.

"No roads led to where I was. It took the driver almost three hours to navigate the Land Rover, until the path became too rough. The two policemen and Father then left the driver behind and walked along narrow paths. It took them an hour to reach the area where I was. But they were unable to locate the exact spot. Father shouted my name many times."

Amina paused and slowly shook her head.

"I thought I heard voices and imagined men with spears. And I thought I saw them running towards me... Their spears went up and down as they ran. I could hear their feet stamping the ground. They came close... I could see their gritted teeth... One of them grabbed me hard...Next thing I remember I was on a clean bed.

"Father later told me that when he and the two policemen came close, they could hear me crying, 'Uncle, please don't kill me! Please, don't!'

"I moaned and talked gibberish about spears and daggers and water. The two policemen climbed the tree, and I talked louder and louder. When one of them grabbed me, I screamed and passed out.

"The policemen didn't think I was going to make it. They carried me to the Land Rover. Father was too tired. When we reached the town, I was immediately handed over to a small clinic.

"For two days, I lay unconscious. When I finally came to, I was shocked to find myself on a bed with clean sheets, a clean blanket, and a soft pillow. A woman was watching me. She looked like my mother. *Was I dead?* I looked through the open window and saw the rising sun. *No, I wasn't dead...*'Where is my father?' I cried.'Where is the baby?'

"...The police took a report from Father, but there was nothing they could do because the supposed crime had happened well outside their district...We stayed in that town for only one week. Father managed to sell the gun. We then traveled from town to town on trucks along bumpy roads until we reached Las Burgabo...

"We got away!"

Amina paused and, once again, began shaking her head slowly from side to side.

"Father never really got over the tragedy. As time went on, it pained him more and more. He never really forgave himself for abandoning the other half of his family... And he hurt so much that some nights he tossed and rolled and screamed in his sleep... He became a bitter man.

"I know what I will now tell you will shock you even more. But I must tell you the complete story."

Amina paused and waited for Ali to digest what she had told him and to allow him to prepare himself for what was to come.

A bizarre melange of emotions swept over Ali. The mother, the brother, and the sister he had never known had met a fate much worse and much stranger than he could have imagined. At some level, however, he was glad he had finally learned the story of his family. At any rate, he had never believed the story of his family was a sunny one; but knowing, however unpleasant, gave him a sense of completeness. He finally understood the reason he had, until now, been kept in the dark. His father and Amina had conspired to spare him the deep trauma the revelation would have caused him in his childhood. His admiration of his father and his sister soared to new heights. Amina had displayed grit, perseverance, and fortitude throughout an ordeal that could have vanquished many a man or woman.

With such feelings and thoughts running through his mind, he dismissed Amina's caution that what she was about to relate was going to be even more painful.

What could be more painful than what she has already told me? he wondered.

Amina coughed and held her chest. He waited for her to catch her breath. "Do you remember what we were told when Father died?" Amina asked.

He felt as if an electric spark had shot through his body. The two had never discussed that sad moment. For both of them that story was taboo.

His eyes widening, heart pumping faster and harder, and feeling shortness of breath, he replied, "How could I ever forget that accursed day?" He was now anxious to hear what Amina had to say.

"I never believed that Father died naturally on his way back from that trip. In fact, I knew he wasn't heading where he told me he was heading. He had always felt guilty for not fighting to defend his family. And he had finally decided to find out what had happened... Yes, he went to that evil place we had years ago called home. Yes, it was a sui-cidal mission. Yes, he met the same fate Mother and the other two children had met. Perhaps, he wanted to join them and be with them forever. Perhaps, they are together in God's heavenly hands."

This was too much to take. He held his reeling head.

He had never known his mother or his other siblings. And, as painful as their tragic end proved, it could not compare with the loss of his father. To him, motherlessness was a dismal void that had been there for as long as he could remember. But the loss of his father was the violent loss of his own once happy, secure, and loving self. His father had been an extension of him, or rather he had been an exten-sion of his father. His father had been the truth that anchored him to life. In losing his father he had lost himself, and his entire life after that became a desperate search for his identity and belonging. Motherlessness gave him a persistent dreary feeling; fatherlessness was like an open wound that refused to heal and that was very painful to the slightest touch.

Having at last told the story, Amina felt relieved of the terrible burden of the painful secret. Her face loosened as she fixed Ali with a sad, tranquil gaze. Her lips twitched in an awkward smile. She leaned forward and sank onto the mat, face down. He moved towards her and felt her back. She wept and sobbed quietly.

He stepped back and thought, his eyes on his weeping sister. He had always thought of his childhood with some bitterness against his dead father—as if his father could have decided not to leave this world so soon. And this sense of bitterness had always led to a sense of guilt. Now, however, he had just learned that his father had indeed abandoned him and his sister for a long-lost cause.

Ali thought for a moment about what might have been had his father not been so reckless. Then his focus shifted to those who had murdered his father and condemned him and his sister to a life of misery.

Revenge! rang through his mind. His eyes turned fiery. His chest heaved. His muscles tensed. Under the spell of a suffocating rage, he stared into space unable to speak. Neither he nor Amina uttered another word that night.

Ali had difficulty sleeping. The story had come down on him mightily. Every episode of the story played out in his mind many times. He became angrier and angrier until he felt numb. Gradually, he calmed down and in the end became even more resolute than when he had walked off the soccer field.

After a turbulent night, a calm morning came. He ate a simple breakfast and then stepped into the sun. He walked slowly as if to prolong the walk. Hands in his pockets, head down, eyes focused on the ground, he walked lost in thought and without tension.

At last, he knew who he was. He was a Yibir, and he had a past that was his past and a present that was his present and a future that was his future. And he was now on his way to the teashop. There he would decide what to do—one step at a time.

As he stepped into the shantytown, a vicious dog barked at him, its muzzle jerking in all directions as it barked. Ignoring it, Ali walked unperturbed. The dog's bark became a growl and then, having failed to scare Ali, the dog squealed and finally slunk away. Ali now gave the dog a contemptuous look. Just then, he saw people looking at him queerly, whispering to one another and looking away to avoid his eyes. He ignored them as he had ignored the dog. A few minutes later, he entered the teashop, grabbed a chair, and sat down.

In a Somali teashop, one could always grab a chair and sit for hours without ordering anything. A teashop was, therefore, an attraction for derelicts, the lazy, and the idle. But it was also a place to relax and chat with friends and meet new people late in the afternoon and early in the evening.

Now, it being a forenoon, there were few people in the teashop. Ali sat alone and ordered a cup of tea. Holding the cup in his right hand, he took a sip and then looked around. Four youths were playing cards. Two more looked on. Five of the six were smoking. The smoke swirled up and out, forming swarming clouds above the table.

One of the youths noticed Ali and murmured to the others. Almost in unison, they all turned their faces towards him.

"We thought you had left town," said one of them sarcastically— maybe even threateningly.

Ali turned his eyes towards the youth who had spoken and looked at him briefly. Then he looked away.

"Look at this man! He is not even talking!" exclaimed another.

All Ali offered was a stiff upper lip and a straight face. Then, suddenly a loud, sardonic laugh came from a corner. Ali turned to see who it was.

"Gutaleh, are you laughing at us or at him?" one youth asked.

Gutaleh was an old man known to have never worked a day in his life. Supported first by his father, then by a younger brother in England, he had three wives and seventeen children. Distinguished by his prominent jaws, Gutaleh was a man who evinced enormous physical power. But this mastodon of a man was a complete wastrel. A talker and a great trencherman, his sole mission in life was to mate with his wives and to delve into other people's lives.

"Why would I laugh at you?" said Gutaleh. "I am laughing at that fool. In a nocturnal graze with horses, a mule takes itself for a horse!"

Shaking his cane fitfully in Ali's direction, Gutaleh shouted, "Yibir!" so loudly that the ceiling shook. But more significant than the loudness was the way the word *Yibir* came out, which was more telling.

Gutaleh made a face of utter revulsion first then put tremendous stress on the *Yi* as if to condense all the derision he wanted to purvey in this one syllable. The second syllable, *bir*, flew out like spit as if Gutaleh was rinsing his mouth of some foul aftertaste.

"Yibir!" continued Gutaleh. "Yibir, the son of a Yibir shall always remain a Yibir and beget only a Yibir! We opened our arms and our hearts to you and almost made a hero of you. Now, see what you have done and how you have rewarded us, the people who have been so generous to you! A Yibir cannot be anything more than a Yibir. This was decided a long time ago.

"Go back, all the way back, to what you really are. We have been wrong all along to make something else out of you. Gather firewood. Draw water from the wells, and carry it on your back to our houses. Help our women clean. In fact, our women should be the ones telling you what to do unless they think it is beneath them to have a Yibir around.

"See how worn out his cloths and his sandals are. He tries to keep himself clean—I grant him that. He wants to be accepted, but he will soon be what he was meant to be: stinking dirty scoundrel. Look at his feet! They always end up with those feet. I swear I can tell a Yibir by his feet!

"Yibirs are supposed to work for us. They even clean the pits we drop our feces in. In fact, that is what they do best. But it is not wise to have a Yibir around because, by nature, a Yibir is unclean both physically and spiritually. If an Aji man marries a Yibir woman without knowing she is a Yibir, he will still know before long. When the moment of truth arrives, the beast will refuse to rise…It has happened!

"Don't get me wrong. I have never disliked Ali. I just want him to be a good Yibir like his grandfather. His grandfather knew who and what he was. He would do anything you wanted him to do. Sometimes, he even volunteered. What a good Yibir he was! I never heard him raise his voice in a congregation. He would walk a step behind you, and he was always in the background unless he had work to do. Ali's grandfather was a good Yibir. Now, all we want of Ali is to be one good Yibir like his grandfather. Ali should abandon all the nonsense stuffed into his Yibir mind by an arrogant father and a stupid principal…

"Look at him! What a wretch!"

As Gutaleh ranted and raved, Ali first decided to ignore him and take it in stride. But then something about the man's contorted face caught his eye. It reminded him of the growling dog in the shanty-town. *Gutaleh and the dog*! What a wonderful connection!

Ali rose to his full height. Two of the sitting youths rose and stiffened. Throwing caution to the wind, Ali drew closer to Gutaleh and studied his face. All watched Ali's every move. Ali was amused. The barking, the growling, the snarling, and the sheer maliciousness of the dog were all there on this beast of a man's face. *It is true*, he thought, *there is no fool like an old fool*!

Satisfied that the old man could not harm him any more than the dog could have bit him, he retreated and reseated himself on his collapsible wooden chair and resumed sipping his tea.

One of the card players rose to his feet and walked towards Ali. It was Adan the rumormonger, who years ago had gone with Ali and the other boys on the hunting venture. One of the two onlookers slipped into Adan's chair and took his place in the card game.

Adan had dropped out of school about two years earlier and was known as a fixture in the town's main teashops.

"How are you, Ali?" Adan greeted.

"I am fine," Ali replied, relieved that finally somebody talked to him nicely. "How about you? I haven't seen you in a long time," Ali continued.

Adan was a facetious man who bore no ill will or grudge to anyone. He had the gift of gab, which he embellished with levity. But one had to take what Adan said with a grain of salt.

"I was in Hargeisa[3] for two weeks. I came back the day before yes-

---

[3] Somalia's second largest city

terday," Adan said.

Ali was alert to Adan's emphasis on the word *yesterday*. He looked into Adan's eyes.

"I am glad to see you," Ali said. It was an honest statement.

"Let's go out, and I will show you something," Adan suggested.

Outside, Adan was his usual loquacious self. Giving Adan a quick side glance, Ali asked himself, Is Adan weaving a fantastic story? Ali shrugged. Adan was always an interesting character to have around, and Ali needed company right now.

"Where are we going?" Ali asked.

"Not far," Adan replied.

Adan led Ali to the old café, where Ali had worked in summers past.

"You see the man facing the door? The one with the mustache?" asked Adan, pointing to a group of men sitting under a tree.

"Yes," replied Ali, wondering what the point was.

"He is Anissa's betrothed."

A sudden chill ran through Ali's entire body, and he felt considerably weakened. His heart missed a beat. His eyes widened. He looked into Adan's eyes plaintively as if to ask, Why are you doing this to me?

But he fell silent. After a while, he cleared his throat.

"Who is he?" he asked in a thick voice. He felt embarrassed. This was not what he had intended to say. He had wanted to ask, Why are you telling me this? But when he had opened his mouth the other words came out. Deep inside him, though, he wanted to know: Who has taken my love away?

"His name is Jibril Warfa Dualeh," Adan said. "He lived in Saudi Arabia for many years."

Ali studied Adan's face with narrowed, inquisitive eyes then turned and stared at the man.

The large man, Jibril, reclined on his armless wooden chair, his right arm resting on a shiny black cane, and the fingers of his left hand twirling his bushy mustache. He looked rather amused listening to another man. At one point, he leaned forward and whispered to the other man. He ended the whisper with a horizontal sweep of his cane in the air and a loud guffaw, shaking violently as he laughed. He coughed and hawked harshly then spat the phlegm noisily at the base of the tree.

What a huge man! thought Ali before he turned to Adan.

"May Allah bless their union," he said. He tried to swallow but his mouth was too dry.

"Amen!" replied Adan, flicking a hand in the air.

The two then walked back towards the teashop. But before they reached it, Adan stopped and turned to Ali.

"I am sorry about what happened yesterday. You must have had a good reason to storm off the field. People are really mad at you. But they will soon calm down and forget about it and like you again. You will have many more opportunities to redeem yourself," said Adan.

Ali again looked into Adan's eyes. He saw sincere concern. He patted Adan on the shoulder.

"Don't worry about it. I do not care what people think or feel about me," Ali declared.

Adan took a deep breath and said with a cracking voice, "That wicked old man in the teashop…He was talking garbage."

"He said what he really thought, and you know that is what many folks think. I am past caring about it, but I appreciate your concern."

"Ali, when are you going to rejoin the team?"

"*I will never play soccer again!*"

"That is bad because you are a real soccer talent."

"I hope to see you again, Adan. I have to go now," said Ali, smiling warmly. He shook Adan's outstretched hand and walked away.

But just then he heard a call, "Ali! Ali!" He turned and saw a young man he did not know hurrying towards him. He waited.

"You don't know me," said the young man as he shook Ali's hand. "I am Bileh. I work for the principal. He told me to look for you. He wants to talk to you."

"The principal wants to talk to me?"

"Yes!"

"When and where?" asked Ali.

"He is inviting you to dinner at one o'clock this afternoon. Do you know where the principal's house is?"

"Yes," Ali replied, "but can you come and take me there?" He was still smarting from the way he had been treated at the gate of Arraleh's house. "And, by the way, have other people been invited?" asked Ali, determined to decline the invitation if the answer was yes.

"No! You are the only one. This is for you!" Bileh replied.

Ali paused for a moment.

"Did he say why?"

"No!" Bileh replied.

"At half past twelve, I will be at the corner of the post office."

"That is fine. I will be back for you," the young man said.

Chapter 9

The Debate

With about two hours to kill before dinner with the principal, Ali went back home. On his way, he reflected on his present situation. Over the past twenty-four hours, a whirlwind of events had a maturing effect on him but, at the same time, left him disoriented and emotionally drained. What he needed was a strong sense of direction.

What could the principal want with me? Ali wondered. But he knew he could not say no to a man who had been of great help to him, and no one, he mused, holds gratitude better and longer than the needy.

His train of thought shifted to the old man's bigoted ravings at the teashop. He knew he had conducted himself well, and now it seemed strange that he had even wanted to hear the old man out. Barely twenty-four hours earlier, he would have hurled the hot tea in the old man's face and accepted the consequences.

He thought of Adan, and the things Adan had said to him. He regretted all the instances in the past when he had looked on Adan with disdain for his mendacity. With horror and revulsion, he thought of the giant about to deflower young, loving, and lovable Anissa. A wave of sadness inundated him—not because he had lost her but because he felt she would never be happy with the man he had seen. And he could picture the bright, sparkling eyes turning hard and dull, the charming smile fading and turning sour, and the soft, smooth skin withering away prematurely.

At home, he lay down and slept. It was around eleven o'clock in the morning. About two hours later, he stepped out into the blinding sun and walked with quick, long strides, much like his father. Sweat trickled down his neck and wet his shirt. As he approached the post office, he could see Bileh leaning against a wall.

"Sorry, Bileh, I kept you waiting," Ali apologized.

"You are not late. I showed up early just in case you might show up early," Bileh replied, simply. The two walked together.

"The principal's Land Rover broke down two days ago. I hope you don't mind walking, even though it is very hot," Bileh said.

"I don't mind walking," Ali replied.

They walked to the northern edge of the residential part of town and crossed a grassy, dry waterway. They passed the police housing units and the courthouse and the jail and the police station and entered a wooded area of white bungalows, leftovers from Somalia's colonial period. The eucalyptus and acacia trees provided a welcome respite from the searing heat of the sun.

When they reached the principal's house, Ali stopped to take a good look. The white colonial bungalow looked beautiful and majestic. They walked in through the wide-open gate. The principal's green Land Rover was parked in the garage. A servant's outhouse stood to the right. As they climbed the steps, the visit to Arraleh's house flashed through Ali's mind. Bileh inserted the key to unlock the door. There was a click. With the slightest push, the heavy wooden door opened soundlessly. They stepped onto the shiny floor of the parlor.

"We are here, sir," Bileh said aloud. The *sir*, a legacy of British rule, was still in vogue.

"Please, sit down," Bileh said beckoning to Ali, before he proceeded to the kitchen.

Ali sat down on one of four plain chairs surrounding a bare table. The chairs and the table stood on a small brown rug. Indigenous artifacts—a wooden spoon, a wooden comb, a spear, a bow-and-arrow and a shield — adorned vanilla walls. Two large portraits of Malcolm X and Martin Luther King faced each other on opposite walls. A large glass window with diaphanous curtains let in a copious amount of sunlight. The hearth, above which hung the Malcolm X portrait, lent the room a European flavor. Books on various subjects graced the simple wooden bookshelves, and issues of *Newsweek* and *The Economist* lay scattered in sixes and sevens, suggesting a vigorous intellectual life.

Ali picked up the latest available issue of *Newsweek* and started browsing. Then a familiar voice greeted him.

"I am glad to see you, Ali. How are you?" the principal said, as he walked with a friendly smile. He was dressed in a sarong, a long-sleeve shirt and a pair of slippers.

"I am fine," replied Ali, standing up to shake hands with his principal. He was surprised that he and the principal were now about the same height.

"Please sit down," said the principal, looking around. "I apologize for the messy house. I have never been good at keeping my surroundings neat and clean."

"Sir, you told us that Somali boys grow up depending on the services of the women in their families. I don't see anything wrong with your house, though, sir."

"First, stop calling me 'sir;' second, don't flatter me. I want us to have a frank and friendly discussion today—if it pleases you."

Ali became a bit uneasy. Here was a man he held in awe. How could he address him any other way or have any meaningful discourse with him?

There was a knock on the inside door. Bileh's voice came through, announcing dinner. The rich aroma of food wafted into the living room. The principal stood up and gestured to Ali to follow. They moved into the dining room. Here too the furniture was simple. A dining table and four chairs occupied the middle of the room.

A dish of spaghetti, a dish of cooked lamb, a bowl of soup, a bowl of lamb stew and a plate of lettuce and tomatoes lay in the middle of the table. An empty plate, a fork, a knife, and a spoon lay on each of two opposite sides of the table. At the sight of what for him was an enormous amount of food, Ali suddenly felt sharp bangs of hunger.

They washed their hands. But Ali hesitated to start eating because he did not know how to use the knife and fork. The principal put his aside and plunged in with his bare hands. Ali followed suit.

"Don't worry about it," the principal said. "You will learn how to use them."

When they finished eating, they moved to the parlor. There was a knock on the door. The principal rose to open it. Three men came in with bundles of kat, a mild stimulant.

"We have a bundle for you too. Can we sit here? Or do you want to come with us?" one of the visiting men asked. Ali recognized the speaker as the police commander.

"No, I have a guest," the principal replied.

"The guest can come too," the police commander countered. At that point, he saw Ali. A look of surprise came over his face. "Here he is! The man who defied us yesterday!" he said, walking towards Ali and extending his hand.

Ali stood up and shook the man's hand then walked over to the other men and shook hands with them.

"Do you chew kat, Ali?" the captain asked.

"No!" interrupted the principal, rather firmly.

"Then, can we leave you some?"

"Thanks, but no. If I chew kat, I will smoke cigarettes, and I don't want to smoke in front of a young man."

"Then, maybe another time. How about Thursday?" the captain asked.

"Only if it will be on me," the principal replied.

"It will be on me."

"We will discuss it when the time comes."

"It will be on me," insisted the captain.

"All right, so be it."

"*Assalamu alaykum!*"

"*Wa alaykum assalam!*"

When the three men left, the principal closed the door and sat facing Ali. Bileh served them tea with milk. Ali picked up a magazine.

"You can borrow any magazine you like. In fact, you can borrow any book too," the principal said. "You will have little time for them when school starts. But before then, feel free to borrow and read as much as you like."

"Thank you very much, sir. I want to borrow this *Newsweek* magazine," Ali said.

"I told you not to call me 'sir'."

"Sorry, I forgot, sir. See, I can't help it!"

"Well, then, don't worry about it. Call me whatever you want to call me."

For a while, the principal was silent. Ali became restless, taking pains to hide his restlessness.

"By the way, tell me. How are people treating you?" the principal asked. For once, his eloquent tongue was at loss for words. He did not know how to broach his intended topic tactfully. Ali gave the principal a quick side glance then stared down at the table.

"Listen!" the principal continued, "I am treating you like the intelligent and educated man you are. Let me come to the point. Society discriminates against Yibirs…." The principal paused. He felt silly saying the obvious.

"As one who cares about you, I would like to know how the abuse of Yibirs is affecting you," the principal continued. He was relieved and surprised that he had just said what sounded ridiculous to say but needed to be said. He paused to let the words take effect.

"If you don't feel comfortable discussing this subject, you don't have to talk about it, and we can talk about other things," the principal suggested.

Ali became quiet and pensive. The principal waited for him to talk.

"You know, mv people don't talk about their situation to outsiders," Ali said, suddenly feeling emboldened. "We see no reason to trust anybody else. This doesn't mean that I don't trust you—you have always been good to me. But just tell me, what can I gain from discussing our problems with you?"

"We can educate each other. I have never met a Yibir with your level of education. Likewise, you have most likely never seen anyone who is as interested in learning about Yibirs as I am," the principal explained.

Like two warriors, they circled each other.

"I don't see what my education has to do with it. A Yibir with education is still a Yibir. For your information, I have even decided to leave school, because all it has done for me is give me false hopes,"

Ali contended, unintentionally throwing the gates of the discourse wide open.

"The biggest advantage of education is that it enlarges the realm of possibilities," the principal said, somewhat startled by Ali's outburst. "People may or may not respect you for your education; but one thing is indisputable: With education you are better prepared and better equipped to see and seize opportunities. You may not have the same opportunities an Aji boy has, Ali, but you will have more and better opportunities than an uneducated Yibir."

"But, sir, it is not just me. It is all of my people, past, present, and future, who were, are, and will be treated like dirt. And as long as that is true I will never feel happy even if I become wealthy and highly educated,"

The principal started to smile then caught himself.

"I am glad you are not an egotist," the principal said.

"I have no choice in the matter. I haven't been given a chance to be egotistical. I am part of my people. My problems are those of my people. There is one big Yibir problem: Aji bigotry. Ajis see us not only as an inferior race but also an evil race. Ajis treat Midagans and Tumals as inferior too, but they do not see them as evil."

"Haven't you seen that Yibirs show tremendous poise and pride?" the principal asked.

Ali was taken aback by the principal's observation, which he realized might be true.

"The question is, What is to be done? Sometimes I feel that we should flee en masse to another country. We could walk and cross borders; but we wouldn't have a way to sustain ourselves during and after the flight. Plus, it would be impossible to convince our people anyway, as most would rather stay with the bones and spirits of our dead."

"Ali, listen to me. History is replete with groups of people who have stayed at the bottom and on the fringes of society because they lost hope and totally submitted a long time ago. It is equally replete with groups of people who have risen from the ashes of servitude and despair. There is something about the human spirit that drives men and women to attain their best at their most difficult moments. Deep down, Yibirs have remained unbroken and thus have retained the basic human dignity needed to survive and ultimately rise to glory."

"Sir, your argument makes sense, but frankly I have decided to leave school in order to be with my people more, to organize them. The problem is organize them to do what? You have taught us about the techniques of the American civil rights movement. Those techniques are not applicable here. You see, as a group, we have no problem with the law or the state. Our problems are with the minds and the hearts of Ajis.

"You can never imagine what Yibirs go through. Behind every Yibir's stoic face is a crying soul and a bleeding heart. It is not just the present. It is the past, which we can't and mustn't forget and which, as such, is always a heavy burden on our backs. And it is tomorrow, which will only bring us more of the past and the present.

"Sir, you know me; yet, you don't know me, and you will never know me. My pain is mine and mine alone; and the only person I can share it with is my sister, who is always too busy worrying about me to share her own pain with me."

Ali was surprised at his vehemence in front of the principal. He attempted to apologize, but, instead, smiled and waited. He was relived he had spoken, and he felt he had spoken well.

The principal's face grew serious, because the lad had said more than he had expected and said it articulately.

"First of all," the principal countered, "stop talking about leaving school. Without education, your people can't escape the old mentality which teaches that things will never change. A new way of thinking can come only with education, and the more education you have the better."

Flinging his hands in exasperation, Ali said, "Remember the time I worked in the café? Well, I learned a lot then about education and educated people. I used to listen to Hassan and Engineer Osman, and I was really impressed with them. But I now realize they were practically useless when it came to solving real problems. My people don't need intellectuals who, on the one hand, talk loftily about what great

Western thinkers have had to offer Western people but, on the other hand, have themselves very few practical solutions to offer to their own people."

The principal nodded in agreement. He himself had no respect for such intellectuals either. He had to concede this point.

"You make a good point," the principal agreed, " and I hope you won't be the type who quotes Hegel and Kant to argue the simplest of points. I want you to study your people, their history, their culture, their problems, their strengths, and their weaknesses. You should also examine, closely and analytically, how society functions, how the economy functions, what resources are available, and how those resources are distributed. You can then think of what your people can do as individuals and in groups to earn a better living. Your role is to be an educator and a doer who practices what he preaches."

Ali listened with increasing interest. His eyes narrowed, as if to focus on a tiny object. He scratched his head, then rested both arms on the table, straightened his back, and looked at the principal with a poker face.

"Right now, I am learning a lot from you. You are already giving me ideas. But pray tell, exactly what would you do if you were in my place?" Ali asked.

"Yibirs need to engage in some economic activity that can encourage self-sufficiency and, in the long run, create a new social reality. Midgans have become craftsmen and barbers; Tumals have become blacksmiths; Yibirs can become farmers. Aji Somalis in this part of the country don't like to farm. So there is a lot of good farmland here. In the mountains there are springs and streams and very fertile soil, which could produce fruits and vegetables on a large scale. In the lowlands, crops like wheat and sorghum can be grown...

"Who owns the land? Nobody, in particular, owns the land! To be a farmer, all one needs is some capital, a permit from the government, and a readiness to work hard. Needless to say, it is much easier to do this in groups than as individuals. If one group becomes successful, other groups will follow. The hardest part is forming the first group, the trailblazers. Yibirs have enough fallow energy to do the job. They need encouragement and education on the subject.

"When this vision becomes a reality, Yibirs will be economically self-reliant and productive members of Somali society. They will then, slowly but steadily, gain the basic respect that all human beings need to remain human. And, over a few generations, equality can and will become a reality. But it will take hard, organized work on the part of the Yibirs and education on the part of all Somalis."

"Are you saying Yibirs are where they are because they don't work hard?"

"No! You see, in the past, when there was no government, Yibirs couldn't have owned resources and could, therefore, not have reaped the fruits of their own labors. There were no laws that said Yibirs couldn't do this or that. But this made no difference, because the Yibir and his property were defenseless. Now that we have laws and police to enforce them, the situation may be different."

"I don't see what difference the government has made in the lives of Yibirs. To us, it is a government of Ajis and, as such, a foreign entity to us. Why should we trust a government of Ajis?" Ali asked.

"Why not test it? You will have nothing to lose."

"Are you sure we have nothing to lose?"

"No! But as the saying goes," the principal explained, "nothing ventured, nothing gained."

"You're asking us to gamble."

"Not exactly. In gambling, one is under the mercy of pure chance. Here, you have some control over how things can go."

"By working hard?" Ali asked.

"By working hard on something that can make a big difference."

"You also mentioned respect. We don't care what Ajis think about us. We just want them to leave us alone and not get in our way. What makes you think we need Aji respect?"

The principal knew he had to be careful now.

"Let's focus on the subject of economic advancement," the principal said in a slight retreat.

"Good! You have outlined a plan. Makes sense. But, tell me, why do I need a secondary school certificate. All I need to do is read and think and teach and work hard. These require no certificate. Right?"

"Wrong! You will need a certificate for two major reasons. First, it will show you can start a project and finish it. Your certificate will be a great symbol of achievement for you and your sister. Second, society attaches a lot of significance to certificates. Many jobs require a secondary school certificate. What's more, a certificate may come in handy in ways we can't foresee. Get your certificate, young man. It would be foolish if you didn't."

There was a knock on the inner door.

"Come in, Bileh," the principal said.

"Should I serve more tea?" Bileh asked.

"Oh! It is already four o'clock. Yes! Please do," the principal replied.

As Bileh served a new round of tea, Ali thought about the scheme the principal had just outlined. Staying in school did not appeal to him, but he knew it was the right thing to do. The principal's advice made sense. Besides, Amina would be heartbroken if he had dropped out of school only one year short of their glorious goal.

"I will stay in school, and I will treasure all you have taught me today," Ali said. He paused and then added, "We will need you and people like you. Maybe you will even join us as we toil and till the land." A boyish smile graced his face.

The principal, face brightening and breaking into that endearing smile so familiar to Ali, said, "I am certainly glad to hear that. I will help you as much as I can."

The two rose to their feet and shook hands, looking more like partners than student and teacher. The principal opened the door and held it. Ali stepped out with the magazine in hand. The principal then asked, "By the way, when are you going back to the soccer team? I am sure they will welcome you back."

"I will never play soccer again. Maybe I can play soccer on the farm." He smiled and went down the steps and through the gate and then walked into the soft afternoon light.

Chapter 10

Down to Business

For one whole month after his meeting with the principal, Ali reflected on the topics raised during their discussion. He read and roamed the woods and the plains surrounding the town. The magazine he had borrowed from the principal was only a start. More followed. Then it was time to hit the books, of which there were many in the house of a man schooled in the American struggle for racial equality. He developed into such a voracious reader that one rarely saw him without a book or a magazine in hand. And the more he read the more he thought and the more he desired to read.

Then one afternoon, he decided in earnest to begin the struggle to obtain a decent livelihood for his people. With a sense of determination, he walked home and waited for his sister to arrive. He wanted to start with her. He had to start with her because she knew his people better and because she was a resourceful woman.

Night came, and brother and sister ate their simple supper. They were sipping tea when Ali decided to broach the subject.

"Amina, I have a plan for the Yibir community. I want to visit their houses and talk to the men, and I want you to go with me and show me their houses and, maybe, talk to the women," Ali said.

"What do you want to talk to them about?" Amina asked curiously, her eyes sharpening.

"I have come up with a self-help scheme for our people. We can't always live in destitution and servitude," replied Ali, going straight to the heart of the matter.

"Our people live the way our forefathers lived. We don't like how we live; but we have accepted it because there is no way to change it," Amina said with a flat note of resignation. "I wish somebody could do something about it. But I don't see who, and nobody knows how."

"How will we ever know if we don't come up with bold ideas and try them? Are we waiting for a savior from God?"

Amina rose from her recumbent position and sat on her mat. She started to cough. When the coughing stopped, she held her chest and took deep and slow breaths. Her eyes widened and showed excitement.

"You really telling me you got something for us?" she asked.

"Yes," he replied, tersely and determinedly.

Leaning forward, she looked into his eyes closely. The deep, serious look she saw there, the set face, and the firmly clasped lips impressed her. Her eyes brightened, and she adjusted her neck and thrust her chin forward in the self-assured manner that had become so gratifyingly familiar to him. He knew she was in. And he knew he would win; they would both win; they would all win—all Yibirs united in pain and hope.

"You are Father with schooling!" She said with pride, knowing she had just given him the best compliment she could offer. "If you are half the man he was, you will succeed, God willing."

"I have always relied on you, and I have received nothing but total support from you, sister. I hope one day I can show my gratitude," Ali said, affectionately.

"With all the things I have been through in life, I couldn't have come this far without you. You have given me something to live for. I have watched you grow and mature and be a man. Fo—for a time, I was afraid I might lose you. But you pulled through. Now, you are one year, only one year, thank God, one year from finishing secondary school! And you are already coming up with plans! I hope this won't get in the way of your education. Maybe when you finish school you can be a clerk or a teacher, or maybe we can buy a typewriter, and you can sit under a tree in the center of town and type letters and applications for people. Then you will get married and have children, and I will be like a second mother to your children."

She was drowned in an emotional wave. Her eyes moistened and dropped a tear, then two, then three. She pulled up a sheet and wiped her tears away and laughed.

Remembering how close he had been to leaving school, Ali became speechless for a moment.

"Certainly!" he said, "This project we are starting now won't get in my way. I will finish school, and I will find a job, and we will have and do a lot of good things. Let's start this project on Friday night, that is two days from now. I want us to see Gureh and Samatar and Omar and Ismail and all the other men and women we can find."

Amina looked down at the floor and thought. When she looked up, she smiled and said, "I will see the women. I will talk to them, and they will talk to their men. Are you thinking of a large meeting?"

"Yes. That would be the best thing."

"Those who disliked Father may work against you. Don't be discouraged if that happens."

"Hopefully, nobody will dislike me and work against me," he said with a boyish grin, too excited to dwell on negative thoughts.

They talked until late into the night, then lay down to sleep. A few minutes later, Amina rose with a cough. She sat and held her chest; but the coughing would not stop. She opened the door slowly and tiptoed out, closing the door behind her. She then sat down and leaned against the wall until the coughing stopped. About half an hour later she tiptoed back in and lay down to sleep.

Late in the morning, Ali walked into town determined to start his activism among Yibirs. With the wind gathering strength, it promised to be a dusty day. He went into his favorite teashop, sat down, and ordered a cup of tea. When he took the first sip, he opened the *Autobiography of Malcolm X*. He was now a recluse much like his father in his later days. There was a rumor that something in the books had cost Ali his mind. The cynical ones thought he was up to something sinister and felt he should be watched carefully.

This time, he did not stay long in the teashop. He walked around looking for Yibirs. One of the Yibirs was a porter; another was a street cleaner; a third dug pit toilets; a fourth scudded animal skins and stacked them in a warehouse. Others were unemployed, and there were some he didn't know. Those who worked rarely came downtown and chatted in the teashops because they had no time to spare.

So Ali was looking for a few idle Yibirs.

In the next teashop he visited, he found Samatar playing cards with three other men. Wearing a dirty shirt ripped in the back, a faded sarong and a pair of slippers, Samatar sat with his left leg bent so sharply that the foot rested on the chair he was sitting on. Ali looked at the slipper under the table. At the heel and at the toes, it was paper-thin, in perfect match with Samatar's disheveled appearance.

Ali stood behind Samatar and gently tapped on his shoulder. Samatar looked up and lowered his leg. Then, his eyes suddenly brightening, he turned around, stood, and held out his hand. The two shook hands.

"I heard you got a little sick," said Samatar, looking cheerful. But when he saw the book in Ali's hand, a look of concern came over his face.

"No, I am not sick. Are they saying I am getting crazy?" Ali asked, touching his forehead. "I am fine. By the way, how is Halima?"

"Very sick," Samatar replied. Then, noticing the restlessness of his card partners, he added, "I will talk to you about it later. It is really terrible."

"I want us to talk *now*," Ali said, before Samatar was able to sit down.

Laying the cards on the table, Samatar regarded Ali curiously before he excused himself and went out with him.

Outside, Samatar was more concerned than curious. Only a few steps away from the teashop, he stopped and leaned forward to listen to Ali intently.

"Let's go somewhere we can sit down and talk," suggested Ali, smiling reassuringly. "I don't want other people to hear what I have to say."

"Something happened?" Samatar asked, bracing for bad news.

"No, it isn't about a problem. It is about an idea I am proposing."

Frowning a little, Samatar protested, "I am a simple man. I am not a man of ideas myself. Why don't you talk to the elders?"

"I will," Ali said. "But I want to talk to everyone, meaning every Yibir."

They walked.

"Wait! I have an idea," said Samatar. "We can go to your place."

"My place? Well, I didn't think of that, but it is a good idea. Let's go."

Samatar suspiciously eyed the book in Ali's hand. He pointed to it and asked, "What do you need that for? Why do you carry books around all the time?"

"I don't talk to people as much as I used to. So I read a lot because I don't want to feel lonely. Besides, there is a lot to learn from books."

"I don't know how to read or write. Yet, if not for my sick wife, I wouldn't feel lonely. I am the one who should feel lonely, not you."

"Well, I like books."

Samatar stopped and looked straight into Ali's eyes.

"You like them?" he asked.

Ali nodded. Samatar ran his right hand through his bushy hair and said in a sad voice, "Maybe that is what I am missing in my life."

They resumed walking, and for a while both were silent. Then Samatar shook his head and lamented, "I have never been taught how to read or write. Never!" Silence followed.

"Can you find a cure for my wife in your books?" Samatar asked.

Ali stopped abruptly and thought about what Samatar had just said.

"I am not a doctor. You need to take her to the hospital," Ali said, slowly and emphatically.

"I *did* take her to the hospital, one year ago. They said nothing was wrong with her. They don't know anything. Or, maybe they don't care. Maybe one day you will be a doctor, and we won't have to ask Ajis to cure our sick. Be a doctor, Ali. That is what we need. A doctor!"

Ali felt sick to his stomach. Neither talked for the rest of the way. When they arrived, Ali asked Samatar to sit on the only chair in the house. He then proceeded to the kitchen to prepare tea. But finding no sugar, he could only come back and shamefacedly tell Samatar that he couldn't make tea.

"We are not here for tea. Are we?" Samatar asked, still somewhat confused.

"You are in my house. I have to offer you something," Ali said.

"Thanks. But let's get to the point."

There was no way around it. It was time to talk. Ali sat on a mat and cleared his throat.

"Lately," Ali said, matter-of-factly, "I have been thinking about a way of improving our people's living conditions." He paused and looked straight into Samatar's eyes to gauge his reaction.

"I am listening," said Samatar, assuming an air of serious concentration.

"We need a new way of looking at things," Ali continued, " and a boldness to take real steps to change our reality. I am proposing that we Yibirs pool our resources and go into farming. As you know, there is a lot of virgin land in the mountains and in the plains."

Samatar's concentration and interest visibly waned.

"Ali," he said, "you may come up with the best ideas in the world. But right now, all I am looking for is a cure for my wife. I am all my wife has, and she is all I have. But I can't help her!"

Ali knew Samatar was talking sense. Caring for a sick wife was a fulltime occupation, physically, mentally, and emotionally.

"I will go with you to the hospital, and I will talk to the doctor in charge. Let's go right now," Ali suggested.

Samatar immediately rose to his feet, his face showing the anxious optimism of a desperate man. They stepped out. Ali latched the door, locked it, and pulled at the lock. He then pulled at it five more times. Each time it held, and each time he thought this would be the last time. He took five steps, stopped, struck his palm on his forehead and returned to the door. He checked the lock five more times then joined Samatar who waited eagerly. But just before reaching Samatar, Ali had one more nagging doubt: D*id I lock the door?* "Well," he said to himself, "I will just have to live with it for the rest of the day."

The two Yibirs hurried to the hospital, a large sprawling complex of wards, offices, exam rooms, one simple lab, an x-ray unit, and stores united by an enclosing fence. Directly they reached the hospital, Ali approached a nurse. She recognized him and seemed glad to meet him.

"We are looking for Dr. Mohamed," said Ali. "This man's wife is seriously ill."

At the mention of Dr. Mohamed, the nurse gave a start. She then stepped forward and whispered, "Haven't you heard?"

"Haven't I heard what?" Ali asked.

Furtively, she looked left and right. Then, in a barely audible voice, she said, "Dr. Mohamed was arrested two nights ago. The NSS[1] took him in the middle of the night…People said he was beaten on the way. We don't know where he is being kept."

Ali was shocked. He wanted to say something but thought better of it. Nobody wanted to show sympathy to a man in the hands of the NSS.

"What about you? Can you help us?" Ali asked.

"You've said this man's wife is ill. Has she been here before?"

"I brought her here one year ago. They told me nothing was wrong with her, which wasn't true. Nobody examined her. They just looked at her and asked her questions," Samatar complained, his voice thickening.

"Bring her in tomorrow and ask for me. My name is Fatima. It would probably help if Ali could come with you."

"Certainly. I will come with them," Ali promised.

A moment of silence followed. Fatima eyed Ali tenderly, her white and even teeth showing through full lips parted in a soft, affectionate smile. He looked back at her and saw the tenderness in her eyes. A vague feeling of uneasiness came over him. He looked away quickly and started to go.

"I have a question to ask you," said Fatima, addressing Ali.

He stopped and stood before her, looking curious.

"I hope I can answer it," he said.

"Will you go back to the soccer team?"

He shook his head from side to side and said, "No!"

With that the glow in her eyes dimmed, slightly but visibly.

He said, "Thank you," and walked towards the door to join Samatar. But before he reached the door, Fatima hit him with another

---

[1] The National Security Service

question.

"Are you aware of tomorrow's wedding?" she asked.

"What wedding?" he shot back.

"Anissa is being wed tomorrow night!" Fatima said in a husky voice and a subdued tone.

He jumped a little and gave her a startled look. Sad and bitter, he looked at the ground. When he raised his head, he eyed Fatima suspiciously before .pirouetting on his left foot and walking away wordlessly.

A few minutes later, the two Yibirs found themselves in the center of the town. It was high noon and getting warm and dusty. Ali turned to Samatar.

"Tomorrow morning the two of us will take her to the hospital. I will be at your house early," Ali promised.

"I pray to God they will find a cure! We will wait for you," Samatar said, his eyes looking glassy.

"By the way, can she walk?" Ali asked.

"Only slowly and with pain."

"May Allah give her health!" Ali prayed. It was all he could say.

They parted. Ali headed home. As he walked and thought about Halima, he remembered what he had set out to do that morning. As far as his plan for the day went, he had accomplished nothing.

At home, he took a short nap until Amina arrived and served him lunch. He went back to sleep. When he awoke, at about three o'clock in the afternoon, he set out to the skins warehouse where Omar worked. But first, he stopped for a cup of tea in a teashop. Then it was almost four o'clock—time to go and see Omar. He crossed several narrow streets until he came to an old section of the town. The warehouse was located near a station for westbound trucks.

He asked a man standing by the door if Omar was in the warehouse. "Yes," he was told. He waited outside. A breeze blew gently and from time to time brought with it a repugnant waft. Half an hour later, Omar was still in the warehouse. Ali sat on a rock under a tree.

The rock felt hard and rough against his hamstrings, and being a tall man, his legs were bent at a sharp angle. After about twenty minutes, he stood up, stretched his legs, and leaned against the tree trunk, putting his weight on the small of his back. For fifteen more minutes, he waited. Then Omar came out.

"Aliiii!" Omar exclaimed in his deep voice, as he raised his right arm high and his face broke into a broad smile.

Marveling at Omar's broad shoulders and thick biceps, Ali put out his hand. Omar brought his huge right hand down and extended it to shake Ali's hand, with a rather strong grip. Ali felt the jarring impact of Omar's strength from his coarse hand. It was a warm handshake—the kind of a handshake Omar saved for people of his kind. The enthusiasm of the encounter desensitized Ali to the otherwise unbearable stench from a man who had just finished his day's work in a warehouse of raw hides and skins. They embraced affectionately.

"Can we go to a teashop and talk over tea?" Ali asked.

"I don't go to teashops after work," Omar replied. "Not smelling like this."

"Then, where can we go?"

"We can go to your house or to my house," replied Omar, looking excited and eager for a conversation.

"You are tired. I will go with you and wait for you until you wash and relax a bit," Ali said.

Omar worked ten hours a day, every day of the week. No other day would necessarily be better than today for conversation.

"Then let's go," Omar agreed.

The two walked together, holding hands and laughing like children. They headed to the western edge of town, where there was a cluster of shacks. Less than ten minutes later, they were in front of Omar's hut. Omar knocked on the door and, as he spoke to Ali, he raised his voice to alert his wife. There was some movement and shuffling behind the door. Then, after it was unlatched, the door opened with a sharp creak. A piece of wood that served as a bolt fell. Omar picked it up and put it back on the door. In the back of the room stood his wife, modestly covered. She greeted Ali. He returned the greeting.

"She is Asha, my wife and my life and my eyes and my heart and my soul," Omar said.

"Don't listen to him, Ali," cautioned Asha, blushing and smiling.

The house consisted of only one room and an adjoining bathroom. An obnoxious smell of putrid milk and decaying skins hung in the air. At one corner lay three blackened stones arranged in a triangle with a mound of ash in the middle. This was the stove. Next to it lay a small heap of dry twigs.

Omar proceeded to the bathroom. Asha kindled a fire and prepared tea in an old, rickety, soot-covered kettle. Soon smoke filled the room. She opened a tiny window to let the smoke escape. Omar emerged from the bathroom, wearing a sarong and an old, frayed towel draped across his shoulders. He was smiling and humming a cheerful tune.

Omar performed the formal afternoon prayers. When he finished, he raised his hands, palms turned up, and looked up in solemn supplication. He prayed for his parents and grandparents and great grandparents and his family. And he thanked Allah for enabling him to work and feed his children. Omar looked so fragile and so tender in front of God that it was as if he were crying. Yet when he finished, he had a wide grin on his face.

Asha pushed the partly burned twigs into the fire. The fire flared. The water turned, first slowly then violently. The kettle cover danced up and down, and a jet of steam blew through the nozzle and whistled plaintively. Then in a graceful act of mercy, Asha rescued the kettle from the inferno and served the men tea.

They talked about Halima's condition. Ali told Omar and Asha that he and Samatar would take Halima to the hospital the following day.

"I hope she gets the treatment she needs," he added.

"A very nice family," Omar said.

A brief silence followed. Then Asha served another round of tea.

"I heard you walked off the field," said Omar, looking straight into Ali's eyes.

Returning Omar's look, Ali pursed his lips and gave no answer. They eyed each other sadly and knowingly.

"I know. I know," Omar said softly. "You don't have to explain it. I know you couldn't take it anymore. We learn that as soon as we start playing with other children. But it took you a lot longer to learn."

Ali's face tensed. His nostrils flared. His lower lip quivered. And he looked into space, silent and sullen. Then, belatedly, he nodded in agreement with Omar.

Omar's wife, seeing the two men wanted to talk, rose to leave.

"I want you both to hear what I have to say," said Ali, looking at Omar but addressing both of them.

Asha looked at her husband questioningly. Omar's face broke into a broad smile.

"Stay, my beloved. Stay. For, if you step out, my mind and my heart will be with you, and I won't hear what Ali has to say."

"If you keep talking like that, I won't stay," Asha cautioned.

"All right. Just stay, and I won't talk like that. But I shall look. This you can't deny me. Right?"

"Keep looking, and very soon you will get tired. But let the man talk."

"Sorry! I almost forgot about you. You want to talk. Oh! It is just that whenever I look at her I become like a child. Pardon me. Talk, brother, talk," Omar urged Ali, partly still teasing his wife, partly serious.

Ali smiled. It was apparent to him that Asha basked in her husband's affectionate banter, and that they loved each other.

"God wants a family built with love and with obedience to Him, and that is what you have. I like it," Ali said.

"Then maybe you should get married," Omar shot back.

Omar's comment struck a chord. Ali stiffened and looked hurt—the very mention of marriage chafed him. He shook himself slightly, ran his fingers through his bushy hair, and then started talking.

"I have come to you with an idea concerning all the Yibirs in Las Burgabo. We have to change the way we think and the way we live. I think we can own land and be farmers. We can live off the land and perhaps become self-sufficient in the end. We can pool our resources, both human and material, and ask the government for land. As you know there is an abundance of fertile but uncultivated land in the mountains, valleys, and plains. All we will need is courage and the will to work hard."

Sitting cross-legged on a mat, Omar listened carefully. Asha, sitting opposite her husband on the dirt floor, listened carefully too.

"Ummm…," groaned Omar when Ali finished. For a while, Omar rocked back and forth looking pensive. He then turned to his wife.

"What do you think?" he asked.

"You know what I think," Asha replied, vehemently. "I would sacrifice my life to secure a bright and honorable future for my children. For God's sake, listen to what the boy is saying! He is talking sense, real sense, and all he needs is men, real men, to make it real."

Asha's transformation, from a modest wife to a spirited advocate of the Yibir cause, surprised Ali. His eyes were drawn to her.

"We need women too, cousin. Real women to make it real," Ali said, his eyes still fixed on her.

"If it were up to us women, things wouldn't be the way they are. No woman can endure seeing her husband ridiculed or her children treated like pigs," she lamented.

Pigs! thought Ali, suddenly remembering the five little piglets. A lump rose in his throat, and the expression in his eyes softened.

"I have a job that makes me stink, and I am paid very little for it. But I earn more than any other Yibir in town. I can feed my family. Yet I would sacrifice it all for a chance at a better future for my two children. My wife is right," Omar said. Turning to his wife with glowing eyes, he added, "This is why I married you, darling."

"Can we hold a meeting Friday night?" asked Ali, trying to seize the moment.

"Ummm…" said Omar, bringing his hand to his forehead and biting his lower lip.

Just then they heard muffled giggles and the voice of an adult female. There was a knock on the door. Asha rose and unlatched the door. Two small children, a boy and a girl, stormed in, followed by none other than Amina. The adults looked at one another in surprise, and the children exploded in laughter. When the children saw Ali, they stopped laughing. Their bare feet were crusty and white with dust. The girl went to her mother and snuggled in her lap and bosom. Eyeing Ali questioningly, she whispered in her mother's ear. The boy, on the other hand, stood silent, right arm held behind his back. The toe of his right foot scratched his left ankle lazily. His eyes looked innocent and inquisitive at the same time.

"This is my son, and that is my daughter," Omar said, proudly pointing to each child. He then turned to the children and ordered them into the bathroom one at a time.

"Wash your feet and your faces," he instructed. "Oh! I forgot to tell you. This is Ali, your cousin and Amina's brother."

The girl whispered in her mother's ear again. The mother smiled and said, "They know him. But they didn't know he was a cousin."

The boy proceeded to the bathroom.

"So you have beaten me to it! There is no need for me to repeat what you have said," said Amina, addressing her brother.

Before Ali could respond, Asha spoke.

"My husband and I are with you all the way," she declared, her face showing the tenacious determination Ali had at times noticed in his sister.

"Good!" Amina said. "I have been to Musa's and Ismail's houses. As you know, Musa has been bedridden for quite sometime, but he is in favor, and his wife Awrala is in favor too. This means their adult children and their families will be in favor. Ismail was not home; but I talked to his wife. She is in favor."

Nodding in approval, Omar cautioned, "It is very important we include Gureh, the old man. He may look like an old pauper and a half-crazy tramp, but we must consult him if we really want this idea to take hold. There is a side of him neither of you knows about."

"So be it. We are not excluding anybody," declared Ali, throwing his arms wide open. "You can talk to him."

"When and where can we meet?" Omar asked, his face all business.

"Our place," Amina said promptly. "Let's make it Friday night. This is what I told the other people."

"Agreed," said Omar, stealing a quick look at his wife.

Ali and Amina stood up. Ali turned to the children and asked, "Do you go to school?"

The two children looked at one another and said nothing.

"Their father wants them to go to school, but I object. I can't stand my children taking ridicule everyday," Asha said, with a sense of defiance. Obviously, the question of school pained her.

Ali shook his head. "They will be ridiculed anyway. But, believe me, they will be a lot stronger if they become educated," he contended. But then, an uneasy feeling of incertitude ran through him. Was he really better equipped to withstand ridicule than unschooled Yibirs? He did not think so.

"Just send them to school," he advised.

Amina and Ali proceeded to the door and stepped into the cool, dark night.

On Thursday morning, Ali stepped out early and headed toward Samatar's shack. A little later, he knocked on the door. Samatar opened the door and led Ali into a poorly lit room. It took time for Ali's eyes to adjust to the dim light. The outline of a frail woman on her side came to view.

"Halima, this is Ali," Samatar said quietly.

Halima stirred and, with a great effort, propped herself with both arms and sat up. A faint smile showed on her face when she saw Ali.

"Do you want another cup of tea?" Samatar asked.

Shaking her head slowly, she replied, "No. I don't want to throw up."

"She had a roll of *kidar* last night and a cup of tea this morning. How can she live like this?" Samatar complained.

Halima rose and dragged herself to the bathroom slowly and quietly, like a plodding ghost. When she came out, her face looked shinier. She turned toward her husband and asked, "Haven't you served him tea?"

"S—sorry. It slipped my mind. Have a cup of tea, Ali," stammered Samatar.

"No. We have to hurry," Ali protested. "I have already had two cups of tea this morning."

"Then let's go," Samatar said, as he opened the door and held it wide for Halima and Ali.

Ali stepped outside first. Halima followed, with the caution of a baby taking its first steps. But she immediately recoiled and covered her face against the blinding sun. She stood still until she was confident her legs would support her and her eyes could take the sun. It was then that Ali saw the magnitude of Halima's physical debility. She took a step forward and swayed a little. Samatar rushed to her side and put his right arm around her shoulders to support her. She shook his arm off and turned to face him, her head held high and her mouth pursed tight, as if to say, " How could you?"

She took one short, firm step, then another, then another. Almost a hundred yards later, she held her abdomen and doubled over in pain. Instinctively, but most unwillingly, she sat down on the dusty ground in the middle of the street. Samatar sat beside her, both their faces suddenly expressionless. Halima's illness had been their pain and their secret, and they wanted to keep it so. But now they were out in the open. People could see them.

"Listen. I will hurry to the hospital and ask for a car. Move to the shade of that tree and wait for me," Ali advised. Samatar and Halima did not answer.

Ali took the athletic giant steps of his father and reached the hospital quickly. He went straight to the nurse he had met the day before and asked her for help. She was more than happy to do so. She ordered the driver of a Land Rover to follow Ali's instructions. Within five minutes, Ali was sitting beside the driver, as the Land Rover sped into town.

They found the husband and wife sitting in the shade of the tree: she holding her abdomen, he his head. Samatar and Halima saw the Land Rover come to a stop and looked up in consternation. *A Yibir riding in the front of a government vehicle!*

Ali opened the door and jumped off. "Let's put her in the front," he said to Samatar. The two helped Halima to her feet and put her in the front seat, beside the driver.

"Get in after her!" Ali said to Samatar. Samatar sat next to his wife. Ali hopped onto the back of the truck. It was the first time Samatar and Halima had ever ridden in the front seat of a vehicle.

Halima walked into the hospital supported by her husband. Ali followed. The nurse met them and asked a few questions before she took Halima to the one remaining physician available. Ali and Samatar waited outside the doctor's office. Twenty minutes later, Halima was helped out of the doctor's office and eased to the floor. Then the doctor called Samatar and Ali in.

"Her condition is grave," the doctor whispered, "and I am sorry to tell you that we don't have the facilities or the medicine to help her. Even our X-ray machine is broken. She needs to be taken to Mogadishu for examination. I believe with proper treatment she can be cured. All I can do is give her pain medicine. I will give her as much as I can."

The doctor paused and stared into space before turning to Samatar and ending with a terse, "I'm sorry."

"Can't she at least be kept in the hospital?" Ali asked.

"If we can't actually treat her, how can that help?" the doctor countered.

"She will at least not starve to death," Ali snapped back, and immediately felt sorry for his brusqueness.

"We don't keep patients just to feed them. But, Ali, I will do that. We will admit her now."

"Sorry. I spoke rudely to you, doctor," Ali apologized.

"Don't be sorry. You are acting boldly for a good cause," the doctor said as he rose from his chair.

Less than an hour later, Halima lay in bed in the women's ward. Ali turned to the doctor and the nurse and thanked them profusely, as Samatar stood by stupefied.

Chapter 11

The Night of the Howling Wind

Thursday afternoon, Ali awoke to the boisterous voices of women entering the house. A hush fell over them at the unexpected sight of a topless man. They stopped, reflexively, and stepped outside. There were four of them, and they carried pillows and rolled mats.

"Come on in," Amina said. "This is Ali."

Ali got up, grabbed his clothes, went into the kitchen to dress and rushed out. He went to town and ordered tea. The muezzin had called for afternoon prayers. Men, young and old, flocked to the mosques. Feeling apprehensive, Ali continued to sit and sip his tea. The fast-approaching meeting was on his mind.

When it darkened a little, he went home. He knocked on the door. Male and female voices came from within. The door was opened. He stepped in and found himself facing Ismail, the man who had been unjustly imprisoned. The two men shook hands and embraced warmly. Looking around, Ali found it hard to recognize the room. Embroidered sheets covered the walls and the mats, and pillows lined the bases of the walls. Taking stock of his new surroundings, he wondered how the women could have created such grandeur. He sat next to Ismail and started a conversation.

Then came the giant, Omar. He embraced Ali and Ismail and proceeded to the kitchen to greet the women. A minute later, peels of laughter issued from the kitchen, followed by the voice of Omar's wife, ordering him out of the kitchen. Omar emerged holding a cup of tea. Soon after, Ali and Ismail were laughing heartily at the giant man's jokes. Now and then Omar took time to tease his wife.

"Don't listen to him!" Asha advised. "He is getting senile at thirty."

At one point, she stepped into the room, rolled a sheet of cloth into a ball and threw it in his face. Omar fell back, raising a leg and shaking with laughter. To others, the lively banter between the couple—in

a country were conjugal affection was seldom publicly expressed—
was quite amusing.

Samatar and Gureh and three of Musa's sons came in. Then
Gureh's three sons came in. Now there were nineteen people in the
house: twelve men in the room and seven women in the kitchen. The
women served Somali *kibis* with ghee and tea. The men— breaking
into two groups, each accorded one big dish— ate with relish. When
they finished, they engaged in light banter while they drank more tea.

Away from Aji eyes and Aji ears, the real personalities of the Yibirs
came out, feisty and funny. There were no stony faces. The flimsy walls
of the house stood as a sharp divide between two worlds: the depressing outside world and the inside world almost visibly transported
back in time. They had to be cloistered before they could make the
journey, the way an astronaut's cabin is sealed tight before blasting
into space. What was out was out; what was in was in. And the pre-
requisite confinement inside the house was rendered tolerable and
desirable by a sweet sensation of relief and joy. Inside the house, the
Yibirs were reliving a time of freedom, a time of dignity, ambition
and hope, a long-lost time only now coming back to life. It felt good
to be back at home.

All were basking in this prevailing blissful mood when old Gureh
gave a signal. He raised his right hand above and in front of his face,
then turned his head slowly. All hushed to listen. Satisfied that all was
quiet and people were listening, Gureh began to speak.

"In the name of Allah the Compassionate the Merciful, let's read
Surat Al-Fatiha," Gureh instructed.

The men and the women recited the Al-Fatiha chapter of the Holy
Koran. Then, the old man proceeded to talk.

"We are here to discuss a proposal from Ali. He will tell us in his
own words and in detail what he is suggesting to us," Gureh said. He
coughed and grunted and gathered his breath. "We will then start a discussion—as usual from right to left."

Never had Ali addressed a gathering of his elders. In the beginning,
he was nervous. But he soon calmed down and was surprised to find
himself talking eloquently. Because the audience knew the gist of the

matter, he did not need to say too much. It took him about half an hour to finish. Then he felt a wave of relief followed by another of uncertainty.

Gureh gave the men permission to talk. The atmosphere grew tense and serious. Everybody who spoke was in favor of the idea. But there was one major concern: How would they get money?

Not all the men spoke. None of the women spoke. When Gureh realized nothing new would be added, he stopped drawing lines in the dirt and raised his head. He then looked around with a wizened face, on which time and sadness had taken a terrible toll. Again a hush fell over the meeting. And all listed towards Gureh, listening in rapt attention, as if drawn by an unseen force.

Some of the men sat cross-legged. Others wrapped their cover sheets around their backs and shins for support. Some stared down, also drawing lines in the dirt, lines they couldn't see clearly in the dim light. The women sat in utter silence, wishing they could see well enough to watch the faces of their men. But in the semidarkness, the faces of the men stood out like apparitions. Ali's eyes shifted back and forth between the faint flame of the pendant lamp and the macabre faces of the men. Outside, a wind gathered force and began to howl.

Gureh bent his shaggy head. His hoary locks fell to veil his face. For a while, he remained silent. Then he let out a deep, rising moan before the words poured out.

"We were once a proud race…."

With a practiced tongue, Gureh began to tell the story. The silent Yibirs watched the bowed old man and heard his powerful voice. In him, they found a deeply buried side of themselves. He was their collective soul, their collective conscience, their collective voice, their collective heart, and their collective past. And this shared experience—suddenly visceral and powerful— whipped them into one cohesive mass that was now centered on the old man.

Gureh now had the power to steer and teach bleeding hearts and crying souls. In the voice of a mystic, he led the group on a dark trail and into a deep hole of sadness. Gradually, centuries of trials and tribulations began to take shape. The stolid faces of the hardened men and women broke. Tears came and coursed down many a cheek.

"…Ajis reject us, no matter how good we are. We stay at the fringes of society and deal with Ajis only if we have to. We do not show them how we feel, and we never grovel for help. Endurance is our strength. Solitude is our refuge. We seek safety in silence. But we are not made of stone. Yes, we are bitter! No human deserves to be treated like the scum of the earth.

"But this is all the life we know. Ajis do not know us. They see us as a big mystery, and they do not quite know how to deal with us, except to keep us down and out of sight. And out of sight we stay.

"For centuries, Ajis have wanted us to vanish; but here we are, bowing only to God! Let fools amuse themselves. We are inferior to no one!

"I am old—very old. Only God knows how old I am and how many years, months, days, or even minutes I have left on this earth. Think very seriously and very deeply before you act!

"We want to own land. Who will give us land? If the government gives us land, who will protect us from Aji predators? Yes, we own little. But we know how to survive on what little we own…

"Sons and daughters, it will not be easy. Think carefully before you act because we cannot afford to lose."

Gureh paused as if to let the howling wind do the talking now. The faint pendant lamp swung back and forth. On the walls and on the men's faces, shadows bounced and danced eerily. The flimsy walls of the house stood and fought against the howling wind. And the Yibirs wept for their golden past—attuned to a connection between the distant past and a howling wind. Spirits of dead Yibirs seemed to hover around the dying lamp. And the dead Yibirs, who in life had never had a voice, seemed to have found a forceful one in the howling wind. An unmistakable pall of fear descended upon the men and showed through eyes held wide on mournful faces. The women could only lean on the elemental power of womanhood. And Gureh, like a rock, sat motionless.

For the second time in a little more than two months, Ali was having a cataclysmic experience. And if the first was more painful and more personal, this was more like a catharsis and a religious awakening. He looked around him and saw the very picture of condensed fear and sadness.

Then the booming voice returned.

"Sons and daughters," Gureh said. "Scions of the honorable men and women of yore, we will incur God's wrath if we let slip this opportunity to change and be free and live in dignity. My children, go for it!"

Suddenly, the men and the women felt relieved. Suddenly, the howling wind felt like a buoyant tune and a spirited cheering. Here and there, the men sighed and whispered and laughed nervously, their voices sounding husky, their smiles looking sheepish. And from the kitchen came a rousing ululation, stirring and shaking the men to back to life. Now, there was no turning back.

Gureh murmured concluding prayers, and all read Surat Al-Fatiha. Gureh then rose, took out an old turban, and laid it on Ali's head. All the men rose and patted Ali's shoulders. The women ululated again as one of the men, in a deep, commanding voice, broke into a doleful song in praise of life and times of long, long ago.

The next day, Ali felt like a renewed man. The time warp of the previous night had lifted him to a new plain of maturity and consciousness. It was as though he had just won a decisive battle. Physically exhausted, but with enormous emotional energy, he spent the day reading, walking, and relaxing in the teashops. But as night fell, the specter of failure haunted him. Where was he leading his poor people? Was there any Promised Land?

It was time for the ebb and flow of hope. Whenever he built a mountain of logical justification for the scheme, he saw it crumble. Fear would grip him, then anger; and he would start the process of justification again. Ever since his break with soccer, he had been a man on a mission. And his journey to find himself and devote his life to his people's cause had left little room in his mind for his customary bouts of doubt. But now his mind was once again a fair game for waves of incertitude.

Saturday afternoon, he was sitting outside a teashop when he glimpsed Samatar. He called to him, wanting to know about Halima. Samatar walked away quickly and turned a corner. Ali rose and scurried behind him. When he reached the corner, however, Samatar was nowhere to be seen. *He must have run. But why would he run? Is the poor man finally losing his mind? I hope not*, Ali was thinking as he walked back to his chair, unable to make sense of Samatar's quick disappearance.

When night came, Ali went to sleep unusually early. Amina's coughs disturbed him every now and then. When her coughing ceased, he was able to sleep peacefully. But just then, in the middle of this quiet and moonless night, heavy knocks on the door woke him up.

Who could be knocking at this hour? Ali wondered, as he jumped to his feet and stumbled to the door.

"Who is it?" he asked.

"This is the police. Open the door!" a voice barked.

Ali's sleepiness promptly vanished, and his eyes snapped wide open. He shook his head to clear his mind and opened the door. Four policemen stood outside, three with assault rifles pointing at him, and a sergeant holding handcuffs.

"The police!" Ali exclaimed, for once unmindful of his sleeping sister.

"Shut up! Don't make us use force," the sergeant ordered.

Ali knew all four men. One of them had been an older schoolmate. All four men must have cheered for him at one time or another during soccer games. But now, their stares were stone cold, and they were treating him like a dangerous beast.

"Don't worry," Ali said. "I will come with you." He dressed and then calmly held his hands out.

At this point, Amina approached quietly.

"Woe onto me!" she screamed. "Why are you arresting him? What has he done?"

Her frightened, uncomprehending eyes scanned the four faces before her. They looked hostile and unyielding. She made a move to step in front of her brother. The sergeant gave her a hard shove to the chest. She staggered back and fell. Ali lunged at the sergeant, but the three other policemen caught him and wrestled him to the ground. They then handcuffed him and dragged him away. On the ground, Amina held her chest and coughed and looked high up to the heavens.

At the police station, Ali was told that he was being held on orders from the NSS. This meant that he was deemed dangerous to the security of the Somali state.

"Ridiculous! You all know me. Why would I act against the Revolution? Talk to me!" Ali screamed.

But whomever he turned to gave him a cold stare. People he had known since childhood were now acting more like automatons than humans. He was booked and thrown into a dank and dark room reeking of urine and feces. This was shocking and utterly incomprehensible to him. Gradually, a daunting realization descended upon him. And he felt that this was a new chapter of his life the end of which only God could tell.

"O God! What will become of Amina?" he moaned, silently.

The next morning, after informing Sahra of what had happened, Amina set off for the police station. She looked straight ahead and walked at a brisk pace, from time to time pausing to cough and hold her chest. At the station, she proceeded to the lone corporal at the front desk. A huge logbook rested on the desk. She composed herself as best she could. The corporal chatted with another policeman. She waited quietly until she was unable to hold her cough.

"Why don't you talk to the lady?" the other policeman asked, addressing the corporal at the desk.

"Oh! You want to talk to me! I am sorry. What is the matter?" the corporal asked.

"My brother was arrested last night. I would like to see him," Amina requested.

"Are you Ali's sister?" the corporal whispered, stealing a quick glance sideways.

"Yes, I am Ali's sister. Can I see him?"

"What is your name?"

"Amina."

He wrote her name in the book and added a few lines after her name.

"Let me talk to the lieutenant and come back to you," the corporal said. He then got up and walked across the graveled yard. To Amina, the crunch of his heavy boots on the gravel seemed to cheer her up a bit. He knocked on a door held ajar with a rock, entered, and then saluted. After a brief talk, he again snapped into a salute and walked back—this time slowly.

"You can't see your brother today," the corporal said, stretching his pursed lips sideways and rolling his eyes.

"What about tomorrow? Can I see him tomorrow?" Amina asked.

"I don't know when you can see him. I know you can't see him today. That is all I can tell you," the corporal said with a chilly tone of finality.

"Nobody can stop me from seeing my brother if Allah wishes that I should see him!" Amina declared before she turned and left.

Just outside the station, she fell under a particularly vicious coughing fit. She held her chest and hunkered down. A large Somali flag fluttered high in the sky. She looked up and saw the lone white star on the blue flag then quickly turned her head down. She leaned forward, dropping one hand to the ground to support herself, and wept quietly.

Meanwhile, Ali paced the floor of his holding cell unaware that his sister had just been turned away. He was the sole occupant of a small windowless cell. He knew this could be either a rough but short experience or the beginning of a long incarceration. He might stand trial in a week, a month, or a year, or he might just languish in jail and never stand trial. With the NSS, there was no way to know. They could always fabricate a case against him from thin air and produce false witnesses. This was his acid test, and he had to show his worth. He would refuse to bow and scrape before the authorities. Amina was his biggest worry. Could she cope with his incarceration, especially if it turned out to be a long one?

Chapter 12

Completeness

"**Y**our Honor," the prosecutor started, "The defendant Ali Geeddi Samatar has held an illegal, clan-based meeting in his house. He has claimed that some citizens are discriminated against. And he has exhorted those citizens to take matters into their own hands and grab land without permission. This is a slap in the face of our blessed and glorious Revolution of October 21, 1969. Our beloved President of the Democratic Republic of Somalia had years ago banned all clan-based activity. Thanks to our beloved and glorious Revolution of October 21, 1969, we have executed tribalism in effigy in all towns. And our people have resolved to fight with all their heart and all their courage and all their might any effort to resurrect tribalism. So the first charge, Your Honor, is the promotion of tribalism. The second charge is sedition against the blessed and glorious Revolution of October 21, 1969. Your Honor, the Revolution has fed him, clothed him, protected him, and educated him. There are many in the country who have not been as lucky as he. Needless to add that the Revolution's bounty shall very shortly cover the whole land; and every Somali, regardless of clan or gender, shall swim in a sea of cornucopia. Your Honor, Ali Geeddi Samatar has been luckier than many because he has already tasted the fruits of the blessed and glorious Revolution of October 21, 1969. And what does he give the Revolution in return? He incites revolt!

"Your Honor, because of the gravity of these charges, I request the Court to remove all nonessential spectators and personnel from the court."

The judge, an army lieutenant colonel, slammed the gavel on the bench and ordered all nonessential attendees out of the court.

"Have you finished your statement?" the judge asked.

"Yes, Your Honor," the prosecutor replied.

The judge turned to Ali and asked, "Do you have anything to say to that? You should understand that these are very grave charges indeed."

"I have not committed any of the said crimes, Your Honor. Our people…"

"Objection, Your Honor!" the prosecutor interjected.

"On what grounds?" the judge asked.

"What does the defendant mean when he says 'our people'?"

"This is a fair question. What do you mean by 'our people'?" the judge asked.

Ali knew he was being trapped. If he said, "Yibirs," he would be committing a crime right there and then.

"I mean my sister and our friends, Your Honor," said Ali, surprising himself with his creativity.

The judge raised one eyebrow, tapped his forehead with the tip of his shiny pen, and grimaced. Assured that he had wiggled out safely, Ali let out a soft sigh of relief. The judge turned to the prosecutor.

"It is an acceptable explanation. One can have friends, I suppose. I will let him continue."

"My sister and I invited our friends for dinner and for discussions about farming. I believe our beloved President of the Democratic Republic of Somalia has, in his great wisdom, called on us to till the land and be more productive. All we were doing was trying to answer our beloved leader's call. Your Honor, I did nothing to warrant my detention for two months without trial."

For a while, no one spoke after Ali had finished; silence ruled the court. The judge scribbled notes on a book then turned to Ali and asked him if he had anything to add.

"No, Your Honor. I don't" Ali replied.

"Does the prosecutor have any witnesses?" the judge asked.

"Yes, Your Honor," the prosecutor replied. "We have one very important witness."

"Bring him in!" the judge ordered.

With a throbbing heart and eyes fixed on the side door, Ali waited. At last, one puzzle was about to be solved. He was getting a chance to meet the man who had betrayed him. But when the "witness" was brought in, Ali felt sick. A man entered, wearing a new ill-fitting shirt, a new ill-fitting pair of pants, and a new pair of shoes. His eyes were downcast. Ali stared at the man with great interest, but the man's eyes never looked up to meet his. After identifying himself, the man's testimony commenced.

"Can you tell us the story of how the meeting in the defendant's house was arranged and what it was all about?" the prosecutor asked.

The man fidgeted and threw a quick glance in Ali's direction before he started speaking.

"Ali came with the argument," he began, "that a group of people he called Yibirs had been treated harshly and unjustly for centuries. He then proposed a scheme to grab farmland. The meeting was supposed to be a starting point for this scheme. But he presented the idea in such a way that people couldn't really understand what he was leading them to. So they made it clear to him that they wouldn't do anything of this sort unless it was legal."

The witness spoke in a deliberate tone and a low voice. Several times, the judge ordered him to speak up, after which he gave a start and raised his voice. But then his voice tapered off in a whisper. Ali could tell that he had been coached.

"Did the defendant have any accomplices?" the prosecutor asked.

"No," the witness replied.

"Were people enthusiastic about his ideas?"

"No!"

"Were people opposed to his ideas?"

"Most were opposed and made their opposition clear. Others didn't really understand the issue clearly."

"I am done examining this witness, Your Honor."

The judge turned to Ali and asked him if he wanted to cross-examine the witness. Ali looked long and hard at his accuser. He was startled to see the man raise his head and, for a moment, look back at him.

I wonder how poor Halima is doing, Ali asked himself, before turning to the judge.

"No, Your Honor," Ali said. Long resigned to fate, he was now in some way relieved that other Yibirs were not dragged into the mess with him.

"All right. Are you ready with your closing statement, Mr. Prosecutor?" the judge asked.

"Your Honor, Ali Geeddi Samatar has clearly committed a grave crime against our blessed and glorious Revolution of October 21, 1969, and against the Somali people. We have proven the dual charges of incitement of tribalism and sedition against the Somali state. The government, therefore, hereby asks the Court for a combined sentence of twenty-five years."

"Do you have anything to say to that?" the judge asked Ali.

"No, Your Honor," Ali replied.

With a faint expression of amusement, the judge twirled his shiny pen and looked Ali straight in the face.

"Court is adjourned until ten o'clock tomorrow morning. The appropriate sentence shall then be passed," the judge declared, slamming his gavel on the bench.

Two days later, Ali stood with his sister outside his cell in full view and within an earshot of a guard. The lenient judge had given him only a fifteen-year sentence to be spent in the notorious colonial jail of Mandhera. This was the first and only time Amina was allowed to visit him since the arrest, more than two months earlier. They both savored the moment. The two hugged and kissed and laughed together. Amina then coughed and held her chest under the right breast. She looked uncharacteristically sluggish and dispirited. And, for the first time, Ali was gravely concerned about her health.

"Tell me, sister. How are you?" asked Ali, looking into her eyes sadly and affectionately.

"Thank God, I am fine except for minor coughs, which I am sure will go away," Amina replied.

He would have liked to ask her many questions, but the sharp stare of the armed guard discouraged him. They both knew there were things they could not discuss.

"How is Halima?" Ali asked.

"She was transferred to a hospital in Hargeisa," Amina answered, as her eyes narrowed and assumed a plaintive look. "But I don't know how she is. I pray to God that she recovers."

Ali understood what Amina was trying to tell him. He must forgive. He fell silent and thought a moment. Then the guard moved in and the visit was over. The two hugged and kissed again before they parted. The steel door slammed shut, and Ali could barely hear Amina's parting promise, "I shall visit you as often as I can."

Nine months later, Amina traveled to the Mandhera jail to visit Ali for the second time. The journey took two days of actual travel time, four days in all among a people she didn't know. It was a rather grueling trip on a bumpy dirt road.

Ali was made to wait by the gate. From afar, she glimpsed him and pulled herself towards him. He could tell her poise and posture were diminished. Gone was the elegant walk, the noble gait. She walked as if heavy weights held her feet. She fought with all her might to support her feeble legs. And with great effort, she dragged the weighted feet. Not allowed to walk and meet her halfway, he endured the pitiful sight. It was torment for him, but he had to wait. Finally, she arrived and laughed nervously. His arms stretched wide, he took two giant steps towards her. She raised both her hands, open palms turned towards him, as if to say, Stop!

Around her, he wrapped his bony arms to embrace her tightly. But just then, he flinched and, with a sinking heart, let go of her. Her ribs! Fragile and protruding ribs covered with thin skin. Her ribcage felt as if it might collapse. He stood back and watched her. She was all skin and bones. He studied her sunken face. Her cheeks had caved in. The receding gum gave her mouth a beastly look. But the greatest change was in her eyes. Formerly bright and beaming, they now looked hollow and sallow.

She looked at him from head to toe and smiled as if to say, I have made it! But it was a faint smile. Her lips parted, stretched sideways and showed her ghostly teeth. There was a flicker in the eyes—a great achievement. But to hold the smile was a taxing feat. The strain showed on her gawky face. Her lips twitched from the nervousness, and the smile faded faster than it had come. She coughed, turning away and covering her mouth as she did so. And she began to pant. Her lungs gave a wheezing sound. She looked up and faced him to see his eyes— and attempted another smile. He watched her in horror. There she stood, chin thrust forward, as if to recapture her former vim and vigor, or to exhort Ali to complete the journey begun so long ago. Then her face relaxed and her drained eyes gave him that soothing and knowing look of times past, and she knew that he knew. And he knew that she knew that he knew. Then and only then did she manage another smile, which survived longer than the one before.

"Amina, you are very sick. You need a doctor," Ali said, in a thick voice and with a heavy heart.

"I was in the hospital for two months. But there was no medicine. They gave me a leave. They will accept me back when I go home."

"I mean right here, in this town. You need to go to the hospital," Ali said, almost tearfully.

"No. They are all the same. Don't worry, brother. If I die, it will be the will of Allah. I can't escape my fate. I just want you to know that we are trying our best to have you released. Uncle Gureh is now in Mogadishu, trying to see the President and talk to him."

"Gureh! Gureh seeing the President! It is incredible. I would never think he could talk to a sergeant, let alone the President. Where did he get the money to travel and do what he is doing?"

"God willing, you will know in due time," Amina replied.

"How is Halima?"

"She passed away about three months ago."

Ali closed his eyes and said a prayer.

"It's time now! The half-an-hour visit is over!" barked the armed guard.

Amina reached into her purse, took out a one-hundred-shilling bill, and gave it to Ali.

"May Allah bless you for Mother and Father and for our brother and our sister and yourself and me," she said. She then stepped forward and kissed him on the cheek. He kissed her, and they parted.

One dull August morning, almost one year after his detention, Ali was summoned to the prison office. He did not know what to expect. To prisoners, such an imperative was, for the most part, ominous. He came to the office, clad in a prisoner's garb and accompanied by an armed guard. At the door, the guard snapped into a crisp salute and announced that the summoned prisoner was there. The young captain looked up from a heap of papers on his desk. With a poker face, he examined Ali, then ordered the guard to close the door and wait outside.

This is not usual, thought Ali. *How can I be alone with the captain?*

The captain rose and walked around his desk. He stood before Ali and studied him carefully, sizing him up. He then held out his right hand, as his boyish face broke into a wide grin. Ali took the captain's hand, tentatively at first, then firmly.

"Congratulations!" the captain said. " By order of the President of the Democratic Republic of Somalia you are to be released. You have been granted clemency. You will remain in jail for only two more months. Two months!"

A wave of dizziness swept through Ali. He staggered onto a chair and looked at the captain uncomprehendingly. Still smiling, the captain let him be. Gradually, Ali's head cleared, and he was able to digest the good news. He rose and smiled and shook the captain's hand again.

"Thank you," Ali said.

"Don't thank me. Thank our leader," the captain advised.

Ali sat down again, leaned forward, and held his head.

"Captain, if the President has ordered my release, why two more months?"

"Because it's the anniversary of our blessed and glorious Revolution, you shall be released on October 21. What is two months, anyway? A fourteen-year period has been shaved off your sentence, and you can't wait for only two months to honor your Revolution?"

"Captain, it is my consumptive sister. I—I want to see her alive."

"You will see her alive."

"Captain, she needs help only I can give. I am all she has."

"She has been living without you all this time."

"Captain, she is pining away, pining away."

"And you are closing in on the blessed day."

"Captain, she is like a mother to me."

"It is not up to me."

"I know. I can only talk and pray and hope and wait and see."

Suddenly, prison, which until now had been like a home to him, was unbearable. But he had to try hard to keep his wits about him. From morning to midnight, he counted the remaining days and hours. Whereas before he had no hope of ever seeing his sister alive again and was resigned to a dreadful end, he was now in a race with and against time. *One day gone, sixty-one days left! Three days gone, fifty-nine days left! Five days and seventeen hours gone, fifty-six days and seven hours left! O God! Let me see and hold my sister again. Let me kiss her, let me nurse her, let me laugh with her! Let me pray with her!*

Two weeks after the good news, he received a telegram. It was from Amina, and it read:

RECEIVED NEWS. GOOD HEALTH. WAITING FOR YOU.
AMINA

He held the telegram and read it over and over again until the letters looked fuzzy and crooked and tears streamed down his cheeks. The tears surprised him—he had thought his lachrymal glands and ducts had dried up long ago. But he was pleasantly surprised he could shed tears of joy for Amina as she had done for him many a time in happier moments.

Then it came; October 21. He woke up early, very early, and prayed. After breakfast he was handed his bag of cloths and thirty shillings (money accrued for his labor) and bid a curt goodbye. It was that simple. He changed and walked to town, where he pulled a chair at a teashop and ordered tea, just like the old days. A cool breeze blew from the sea as he sipped his tea and mused. Then, he saw a friendly jail guard walking hastily towards him, a slip of paper in hand. Wearing a curiously nervous smile, the guard handed Ali a telegram.

The initial shock was profound but short. A chill sped throughout his body. And he could feel a sudden heaviness in his bones and in his stomach. His eyes turned to the telegram one more time. There was no mistaking it. Amina had left the world. He had come so close to a blissful reunion. If not for the vulgar delay in his already granted release, he might have been at her side in her last hours on earth. And he might have been able to bid her farewell and give her a final kiss. But now, somewhere in his cavernous mind, he would always be sitting in that teashop, sipping tea and looking forward to meeting his sister. And he asked himself why things had to happen this way.

Heading east, the Nissan truck rumbled through the plains along the rutted road. A thick ball of dust trailed closely. From time to time, the more than twenty people who slouched lazily on the back of the truck were jolted back to life by a cruel bump or an abrupt shift in gear. Ali sat looking around like a tourist, awed by the vast expanse of land.

Open land frees and stimulates the mind. Its smooth continuity presents a vivid sense of time: past, present, and future. In the plains, man sees farther, stands taller, roams wider, and feels, thinks, and talks like a poet. And so like a bird perched high, Ali gazed far and wide, feeling and listening to the rhythmic beating of his grieving heart. And the pallid October afternoon began to fade.

Night fell upon the plains. Tossed and rocked around countless times, the passengers had long come to peaceful terms with their crammed nooks. The stars shone bright in the moonless sky. A cool wind blew and an elderly man sang a hymn to God. Ali looked up and gazed far out into the starry firmament. *How would it feel to fly and swim among the stars? Would I be welcome?* His restless self had always sought and received solace from the stars. For on this earth there is no grander sight than a starry sky in a clear and moonless night. The stars twinkled and moved west, slowly and majestically. He dozed off and dreamed.

Amina's beaming face came to view. "I found them…They are all here… Don't be sad…I am happy Ali, I am happy…." And he saw his father's back moving away, never to return and heard Gureh's booming voice, "We were once a proud race…."

At dawn, he woke up and saw the morning star slowly turning golden and rising higher and higher, ushering in another day.

He had dared to dream and reach for more only to fall flat on his face. And now he lay curled up much like his sister on one portentous day about ten years earlier. Around him lay humans he could not relate to. As far back as he could remember, he had dealt with Ajis. Yet he did not know them. Ajis stood as an impenetrable jungle and an unsolvable enigma. He had spent his life peeping through a window into the Aji world only to learn that it was an exercise in futility. It was time to turn and walk away.

He had lost all desire to interact with Ajis. He could see them but only as bogeymen; feel them but only as a millstone around his neck; hear them but only as a voice of torment; talk to them but only as one would talk to a mute. And this was not the result of a conscious decision he had made but rather a mental, emotional, and psychological state he had reached. This way he could be with Ajis in close proximity and at the same time totally block them out of his mind. At last, he had his own carapace much like the tortoise he had seen years earlier; he would venture out only when he needed to. This was the essence and the heart of Yibirness, which had eluded him for his entire life. The circle had closed.